"I've nev‌‌‌‌‌‌‌‌‌‌‌‌‌‌‌‌‌‌ life,"
Elizabeth said, desperate to ma‌‌‌‌‌ believe
her. She felt her own tears wet on her cheeks.

"I know that," he assured her, squeezing her a
little to punctuate his words. "I wish things could
be different. . . . I wish Antonia and I—" He broke
off suddenly.

If only Elizabeth could forget everything but
Laurent and the waltz. But she couldn't do it. She
couldn't take another step and pretend that she
wasn't devastated by his engagement. "Laurent, it's
no use," she said in despair. "I can't do this, knowing that you and Antonia—"

A shriek suddenly pierced the air. "Thieves!"
came the countess's shrill, demanding voice.

Elizabeth gasped as Jessica grabbed her by the
arm and said hoarsely, "We have to go . . . *now!*"

Visit the Official Sweet Valley Web Site on the Internet at:

http://www.sweetvalley.com

SWEET VALLEY High®

HAPPILY
EVER AFTER

Written by
Kate William

Created by
FRANCINE PASCAL

BANTAM BOOKS
NEW YORK • TORONTO • LONDON • SYDNEY • AUCKLAND

RL 6, age 12 and up

HAPPILY EVER AFTER
A Bantam Book / September 1997

Sweet Valley High® *is a registered trademark of Francine Pascal.*
Conceived by Francine Pascal.
Produced by Daniel Weiss Associates, Inc.
33 West 17th Street
New York, NY 10011.
Cover photography by Michael Segal.

ISBN: 0-553-57068-4

Published simultaneously in the United States and Canada

Bantam Books are published by Bantam Books, a division of Bantam
Doubleday Dell Publishing Group, Inc. Its trademark, consisting of the
words "Bantam Books" and the portrayal of a rooster, is Registered in U.S.
Patent and Trademark Office and in other countries. Marca Registrada.
Bantam Books, 1540 Broadway, New York, New York 10036.

PRINTED IN THE UNITED STATES OF AMERICA

OPM   0 9 8 7 6 5 4 3 2

To Anna Smith

Chapter 1

"This is a nightmare!" Jessica Wakefield moaned. She tossed her blond hair to one side and stifled yet another round of tears that threatened to overflow her eyes. "We were supposed to have the greatest summer ever, and now we may never even see daylight again."

Jessica rubbed her wrist where the iron cuffs chafed her skin. She and her twin, Elizabeth, were chained to a dank and moldy stone wall in the dungeon of the Château d'Amour Inconnu on a remote island in France.

Under most circumstances Jessica would have been happy, considering the way her lavender ball gown fit snugly around her body, showing off her curves. Its fluffy skirt billowed to the floor around her legs, and elbow-length white gloves gave her a sophisticated elegance. But what good was a beautiful gown when no one could see her?

Upstairs the prince and princess de Sainte-Marie were hosting a glittering ball, with music and dancing and champagne. That's where the twins would have been if they hadn't been accused of stealing a valuable jewel.

"Oh, why did this happen?" Jessica wailed.

"Well, it wasn't my idea to come to Europe as an au pair this summer," Elizabeth grumbled. "I wish I'd never left Sweet Valley!" She wrapped her free arm around the fitted bodice of her stunning white ball gown. Her blond hair was arranged in large curls atop her head, with a single strand dramatically framing the right side of her face.

"Me too," Jessica said. It seemed as if they'd been away from their friends and family back in California for years instead of weeks.

Jessica knew she'd bullied Elizabeth into accepting the au pair position, but she had imagined them living like princesses at the château. Instead they had been thrown in the dungeon like criminals. She pounded her fist on the little cot in the cell with sudden vehemence. "I could kill Jacques for giving me that stupid emerald!" she cried in frustration.

Jacques Landeau, supposedly the future duke of Norveaux, was the sexy young Frenchman Jessica had met while they were traveling from Paris to the royal château. He was tall and incredibly handsome, with dark brown hair and almond-shaped, deep brown eyes. He swept her off her feet with his sultry French accent and flowery words, and when he gave her an emerald pendant, she just knew she was in love with him.

Elizabeth shot her a scathing look. "You would have to fall in love with a jewel thief," she said accusingly. "Why didn't you listen when people told you there was no such place as Norveaux?" Her tone turned sarcastic. "Jacques Landeau, the duke of Norveaux. *Please!*"

"You don't know for sure that he stole it!" Jessica insisted. "And besides, I'm not the only one who fell for the wrong guy. Since when do you steal other girls' boyfriends?"

Elizabeth winced, and Jessica smiled triumphantly. Her sister had been more than a little swept off her feet by darkly handsome Laurent de Sainte-Marie, eldest son of the prince and princess. Because Elizabeth and Jessica were responsible for taking care of his younger brother and sisters, Elizabeth and Laurent had been thrown together more than once. Their chance encounters had quickly become planned rendezvous.

Jessica had actually encouraged the relationship all along. After all, her sister deserved an incredible guy like Laurent. Why should a silly little thing like his fiancée get in the way? But now Elizabeth was attacking Jacques, and Jessica wasn't about to sit around and be the only person who felt lousy.

"He said he loved me," Elizabeth said, and Jessica heard the tears in her sister's voice. "I was so sure he

3

was telling the truth. I don't understand how he could tell me that while he was engaged to Antonia."

Antonia and her mother, wicked and snobbish Countess Doloria di Rimini, had traveled with Jessica and Elizabeth on the train from Paris to the château. Both red haired and green eyed, they imperiously ordered everyone around and expected the first and best of whatever was available, whether food or service. From the start they had given the twins nothing but grief, and it was the countess who finally accused them of stealing her emerald pendant.

"I just want to get out of here." Jessica groaned, shivering in the damp. "This cell is so dark and cold!" There was one barred window in the stout wooden door and another window high in the opposite wall, where Jessica could just see stars in the sky. One dim lightbulb hung from the ceiling, giving off only enough light for them to see each other.

"If we do ever get out of here, I never want to leave home again," Elizabeth said, tugging on the chains that bound her to the wall.

Jessica and Elizabeth were identical twins, but their long blond hair and stunning blue-green eyes were practically all they had in common. Jessica was impetuous and a first-class flirt, not above stealing another girl's boyfriend if she wanted him. Elizabeth was a good student and far more serious. Before they left home, she had had a steady boyfriend, Todd Wilkins, and would never even

4

have thought of being with another guy.

At least Todd and Liz broke up before we left, Jessica thought. *Todd's such a drip, and Laurent is so much more exciting. I'm* glad *I burned the one letter Todd sent her. Elizabeth didn't need the grief!*

Jessica always enjoyed being the more adventurous twin but never hesitated to coax Elizabeth into helping her out when she got herself into trouble with her wild schemes. Sometimes she even thought her sister *liked* to swoop in and save the day.

Only now Jessica's wild nature had landed them in a dungeon, and neither one of them was enjoying it.

"I wish Dad had never even mentioned this stupid au pair job!" Jessica complained, trying to remove some of the blame from herself. She shifted on the hard cot, tucking her left foot under her right leg.

"Just because he mentioned it didn't mean we had to go for it," Elizabeth snapped, tugging at the chains again. The clattering of the metal against the bricks was beginning to grate on Jessica's nerves.

"Why do you keep pulling on those things? Have you suddenly developed some kind of super-human strength?" Jessica asked irritably.

Elizabeth heaved an impatient sigh, as if Jessica had just asked the most ridiculous question in the world. "This château is hundreds of years old. These chains might be rusted enough to pull away," she explained impatiently.

"I never thought of that," Jessica said, and she tugged at hers too. "They feel pretty tight to me."

"Yeah, but at least it's something to do. I can't *stand* just *sitting* here," Elizabeth said vehemently.

"But even if we get the chains out of the wall, how do we get the door open?" Jessica demanded.

"One thing at a time," Elizabeth said grimly. She switched her attention to her leg chain, as if she was hoping it might not be as secure.

"I knew being an au pair wasn't the most glamorous job in the world," Jessica said as she bent down to help Elizabeth. "But I never figured we'd end up strapped to a wall like common criminals. We should be waltzing around that ballroom right now, mingling with royalty."

Jessica gave up and plopped back down on the cot, sticking out her bottom lip in an exaggerated pout.

"I think I'm getting somewhere," Elizabeth said. Jessica watched hopefully as Elizabeth was able to wiggle the bolt that held her foot chain back and forth in the wall.

"Wow, Liz, you were right about this old place," Jessica admitted. "If we can just unchain ourselves and get the door open, I promise you Jacques will pay for what he did to us."

"Don't make promises you can't keep," Elizabeth warned. "And don't forget there's a guard outside to get past too."

"The guard . . . ," Jessica said thoughtfully. She could feel an idea beginning to hatch, and she stood up and approached the door. The guard outside was sitting on a wooden chair that he had tilted back against the wall. He was short, with dark hair, and his uniform was too tight for his paunch. "Why didn't I think of this before?" she wondered out loud.

"Think of what?" Elizabeth asked, still working on her chains.

Jessica whirled around to face Elizabeth. "The guard is a *guy*," she whispered excitedly.

"So?" Elizabeth whispered back. By the light of the dim bulb overhead, Jessica saw understanding light up Elizabeth's face. "You're not serious!"

"Yes, I am. He might be on the old side, and he might speak more French than English, but he's still a guy," she pointed out. "And you know what I can do when I set my mind to it."

Elizabeth shrugged, her hands in the air. "I can't think of a better plan," she admitted. "And doing something is better than doing nothing at all."

Jessica smiled at her twin and turned back to the door. "*Excusez-moi*, monsieur," she began, smiling through the bars. "*Parlez-vous anglais?*" She hoped that he did indeed speak English, because those two French phrases were practically the only ones she knew really well.

The guard looked up at her, his black eyes flat in the dim light. "Yes, I speak some," he said with a heavy accent.

Jessica cast about in her mind for a good question. "Do you know what time it is?" *Lame*, she thought. But he did look at his watch.

"Just after eleven," he said gruffly in his heavily accented English.

"Thank you," she said warmly. Now that she knew he could understand her, Jessica plunged ahead eagerly. "It must be awesome to be a guard in a royal household. Did you have to go through a lot of training?" She hoped that he could see her brilliant smile from behind the bars.

"We are all highly trained," he said, his voice softening a bit. Jessica watched as he stood up and sucked in his gut. *Gotcha!* she thought triumphantly.

Now that she could see his full face, she realized he wasn't bad looking. His eyes were actually brown instead of black, his face was smooth shaven, and his full head of thick black hair showed touches of gray at the temples.

"I can tell," she said. "You look like you're in good shape. Do you have lots of muscles in your arms?" Behind her she heard Elizabeth trying to stifle laughter. "Can I feel them?" She batted her eyelashes and smiled even more, stretching her fingers toward him through the bars.

The guard came a little closer, looked her up and down, and locked eyes with her. Jessica kept her expression as innocent as possible.

"American girls, ha, so forward!" he sneered. "No, you cannot feel them. Sit down and shut up if you don't want to get into more trouble!" He snorted once before sauntering back to his chair, where he sat heavily and pulled out a newspaper to read.

Jessica stamped her foot in frustration. *Just one more thing to hate about this country,* she thought. She slumped down next to Elizabeth and pouted. "This place is awful," she snapped.

She fought back the urge to cry, but what was the point? They were trapped here in the dungeon, alone and shivering, and no one but Elizabeth was going to hear her sobs. Jessica could feel the cold from the hard stone floor seeping through her satin slippers and making her feet ache.

"At least you tried," Elizabeth said with a sigh.

"It's all my fault!" Jessica wailed, giving in to her misery and beginning to weep, the tears rolling down her cheeks. She tasted the salty tears on her lips and sniffed to keep her nose from running. "Jacques seemed so sincere with his talk about moonlight and French nights," she continued. "Oh, why did I believe him? How could I be such an idiot?"

"I hate to say it, Jess, but I tried to warn you Jacques was bad news right from the beginning. If you weren't such a flirt," Elizabeth accused, "he probably wouldn't have given you the emerald in the first place!"

Elizabeth stood up and paced. Of course, the chain that held her to the wall didn't permit her to go more than a few steps in any direction. She wished Jessica would either stop whining or think of something productive to do, something other than trying to seduce the guard. After all, she *had* gotten them into this mess.

9

"I never even wanted to come to this dumb château. Why did I ever let you talk me into it?"

Elizabeth had turned down an exciting summer job at *Flair* magazine, where she would have learned a lot about being a professional writer, just to come here. She hadn't been totally comfortable about the decision in the first place. Then the night before they left Sweet Valley, Jessica's best friend, Lila Fowler, had given them a big going-away bash at her father's mansion, Fowler Crest. It started out as a great party, but Todd had ruined the evening by breaking up with Elizabeth unexpectedly. His rash decision had come as a total shock to her. He had actually said they should be free to see other people during the summer!

Elizabeth wasn't sure if Todd had severed their relationship because he felt hurt that she was going so far away or if he was already interested in someone else. But his words had broken her heart, and she had lashed out at him. Elizabeth winced at the memory. *He was probably dying to find a new girlfriend after that,* she thought. Just imagining Todd with another girl made her want to sob her heart out.

"Well, what about you, Liz?" Jessica said accusingly, breaking through Elizabeth's sad thoughts. "You didn't exactly make the right choice of guys."

Elizabeth sighed. She couldn't begrudge Todd a new relationship after the way she had acted this summer. After just a few meetings with Prince Laurent she had fallen helplessly in love with him.

"You're right, Jess. But you can't deny that Prince Laurent is something special." She tingled at the memory of how she had burst from the château's maze of hedges that first day only to find the stunningly handsome Prince Laurent practicing his fencing. He had taken her breath away!

The muscles in his shoulders and back had rippled at his every movement, his back glistening with sweat in the bright sunshine. Elizabeth had experienced a weird sense of déjà vu. Later she had recalled a dream she had had on the plane. She had dreamed of Laurent even before she met him!

A few days later a sudden storm forced Elizabeth to take shelter in what she thought was a deserted cottage, but it turned out to be Prince Laurent's hideaway. The tall prince captivated Elizabeth, with his warm blue eyes, thick black hair, and noble, chiseled features, as well as his sensitive, caring nature and great sense of humor.

From the moment Elizabeth met Laurent, it seemed as if they'd known each other forever. He tempted her away from her au pair duties for horseback rides and picnic dinners in the moonlight. Even finding out that he was engaged to Antonia di Rimini hadn't managed to extinguish the fire he'd lit in her heart.

"Do you think Prince Laurent will try to get us out of here?" Jessica asked hopefully.

"I hadn't really thought about it," Elizabeth admitted. "But I do believe he loves me. I can't imag-

11

ine that he would leave us here, if he even knows where we are."

"You're right! Who would tell him?" Jessica whined. "I don't think the de Saint-Maries want him socializing with us in the dungeon while there's a ball going on."

"Probably not," Elizabeth agreed. Her head was pounding from the effort to figure a way out of this dank, creepy dungeon. Her hands were so cold, they were going numb, and she put them under her arms to try to warm them up. "But I bet the countess has told everyone and anyone how she caught the thieves who stole her necklace!"

"I can just hear her now," Jessica sneered. "How can Prince Laurent even think about marrying anyone as disgusting as that Antonia?"

"Laurent is a very dutiful son," Elizabeth said, rushing to his defense. "It's very brave of him to keep with tradition and follow through with his father's wishes." *Even if it's not what he truly wants,* she added silently.

"You mean *stupid,* don't you?" Jessica asked. "No one would ever force me to marry someone I don't love, not even our parents."

Elizabeth couldn't imagine what Laurent's life would be like, married to Antonia. And the horrible countess would be his mother-in-law! What could be worse?

"Stop criticizing Laurent," Elizabeth warned her sister. "After all, it was Jacques who got us into this

12

awful place, but Laurent will be the one to rescue us."

"You don't know that for sure," Jessica pointed out snidely.

"Let's not fight about this," Elizabeth pleaded, suddenly weary of the struggle. She dropped the chains with a loud clang. "Oh, Jess," Elizabeth said with a sigh. "I was right. We never should have come to the Château d'Amour Inconnu!"

Prince Laurent moved through the steps of the waltz automatically and without thought. The music, the decorations, the glittering jewels on the women, all were lost on him. Along one wall of the ballroom, mirrors were hung floor to ceiling, and he watched himself dance with Antonia.

She was wearing a stunning silver ball gown that was cut low in the neck and clung to every curve. Her red hair was dressed with pearls, and a matching necklace adorned her throat. But her scornful expression and uplifted, imperious chin spoiled any beauty her outfit might have loaned her. *How much more beautiful Elizabeth would be in that dress*, Laurent thought.

He couldn't stop thinking about Elizabeth and how it should have been her in his arms instead of Antonia. He couldn't really believe that Elizabeth was guilty of stealing the countess's emerald. At first he'd doubted Elizabeth—he'd fallen in love with her so quickly, and they came from such different worlds. But as the evening wore on, he couldn't stop remembering the sweet, innocent look in Elizabeth's blue-green eyes, from the very first moment she had come to his cottage in the storm. Now he was sure she could never be a thief, and his heart was torn at the thought of his one true love sitting in the dungeon. He needed to get away from this place and these people and find a way to see her!

But one glimpse of his father from across the room reminded him of his duty. He looked down at Antonia's upturned face.

"Are you having a good time?" he asked, not really wanting to know the answer.

Antonia fluttered her eyelashes up at him. Did she have something in her eye? Feeling disgusted, Laurent realized that Antonia's rapid blinking was her idea of a sexy look.

"I've never been so happy in my whole life," Antonia purred. "This is a dream come true, dancing in your arms like this."

"I'm glad," Laurent managed to say, though his voice came out flat and unemotional. All his thoughts were concentrated on Elizabeth. *Is she cold and scared in the dungeon? How can I get her out? I must get away soon to see her!*

Laurent waltzed Antonia past the dais where his parents and the countess were sitting, and he flinched when he saw the pleased expressions on their faces. He quickly averted his eyes.

When he'd learned that his parents had

arranged a politically important marriage for him with Antonia di Rimini, he was devastated. He wasn't sure he wanted to get married at all, and he hardly knew Antonia. Of course, the reason that Antonia and her mother had come for this extended visit to the château was so he could get to know her better.

So far, he knew he didn't feel for her what he thought he should feel for his future wife. He certainly didn't love her! In fact, he disliked her, and he positively hated her overbearing mother, the countess.

Then, when Elizabeth Wakefield had entered his life and turned his world upside down, he knew for certain that his destiny didn't lie with Antonia. He had actually dreamed of Elizabeth before he knew she even existed, when he fell asleep in his favorite spot by the pond one afternoon. But when she showed up at his door that stormy night, he felt as if lightning had struck.

After that, Laurent fell in love with Elizabeth without even trying. Every moment they spent together was like being in his dream, and he never wanted to wake up. His parents believed he would do his duty and marry Antonia. But they didn't know that he was desperate to find a way to spend the rest of his life with Elizabeth Wakefield instead. She had captured his heart, and he had no intention of trying to take it back.

"Laurent, you look a thousand miles away," Antonia complained in her shrill voice, cutting into his thoughts. "What are you thinking?"

"I'm sorry if I seem distracted, Antonia," he said, pushing his memories of Elizabeth to the back of his mind for the moment. "I guess I was just daydreaming."

"About me, I hope." She batted her eyelids again, and Laurent fought the urge to laugh at the silly gesture. He wished he could tell her how foolish she looked.

"Hmmm," he murmured noncommittally. "Well, would you like something to drink? It's quite warm in here."

"Yes, it is. Perhaps champagne?" Antonia led Laurent to a corner of the ballroom where they could sit on a narrow love seat and be partially concealed by a potted plant. He almost groaned out loud at the thought of being so isolated and intimate with her. But he did the right thing by waiting until she was seated before bowing slightly and going in search of the champagne.

While Laurent got their drinks, he let his thoughts return to Elizabeth. His heart ached to think of her in the cold, dark cell of the dungeon. He longed to put his arms around her to comfort her. He yearned to place his lips on hers in a long, passionate kiss. How long did he have to put up with Antonia before he could break away and get to Elizabeth?

When he returned to Antonia, she was waving her fan lazily before her face. At the sight of him she smirked and patted the love seat beside her. "Come sit right here, Laurent," she cooed.

"Your champagne, Antonia," he said, handing her a glass. He sat down as far from her as he could, but the love seat wasn't large. At most he could put only a couple of inches between himself and Antonia.

Antonia smiled and sipped at her champagne, and then she started that repulsive eyelash thing again. "Oh, Laurent, let's not rest too long," she said. She pressed her knee against his boldly. "I could dance all night in your arms with no trouble at all!"

"And I yours," he said automatically. Just then, out of the corner of his eye, he noticed the countess bearing down on them, a gleam in her eye. Antonia was almost tolerable, but Laurent was beginning to believe the countess was pure evil.

Laurent stood up respectfully and gave the countess a slight bow. "Countess. I'm sure you and Antonia have a great deal to discuss, and this love seat is certainly too small for three. So if you will excuse me, please?" He bowed again and walked away without waiting for either of them to speak.

As soon as he left them he crossed the ballroom, ignoring anyone who called his name. He was on his way to the dungeon! Even a few stolen moments with his beautiful Elizabeth would be better than the torture of Antonia's company.

Chapter 2

Jessica opened her eyes to almost total darkness. Where was she? Her cheek was up against a cold, hard surface, like a stone. *A stone wall?* She groaned, remembering that she and Elizabeth were still locked in the dungeon. She must have actually cried herself to sleep earlier, after her frustrating attempt to enlist the guard's help had failed.

As she gradually awoke she became aware that Elizabeth was standing at the cell door, peering out the small, barred window. "What are you doing?" Jessica asked groggily.

"It's the kids," Elizabeth hissed back.

Jessica hopped off the cot to join her twin at the window. In the dim light of the bulb that hung outside their chamber she could see that the door between the hallway and the stairs was open. The guard was looking down at something in the doorway, and

Jessica heard Claudine's voice speaking French. "What is she saying?" Jessica asked Elizabeth, leaning close to her ear and whispering.

"She said they want to see us, talk to us," Elizabeth answered. Jessica could see Elizabeth's eyes bright with expectation and new hope. The guard spoke in a flurry of French, and Jessica was about to ask Elizabeth what he said when Pierre's voice piped up.

"Claudine, we must to speak English, like the au pairs tell us," he insisted.

"Yes," Claudine said. "Pierre is right. English. We want to see Mademoiselle Jessica and Elizabeth."

"No. You should not be here," the guard replied in his own halting English. "This is no place for children!"

"Please," Pierre whined. "We only want *un moment* with them!"

The guard began to try to herd them up the stairs with his open arms. "No, no, no," he said.

"Wait," Claudine cried. "A splinter. My finger. It hurts!"

"Mon Dieu!" the guard exclaimed, slapping the palm of his hand to his forehead. "What next?"

"Ooh, it hurts, it hurts!" Claudine cried again, jumping up and down. Manon, the youngest of the three children, began to jump too, giggling.

"Let me get a flashlight," the guard said, "and I'll try to get it out." He half turned away from the children, and Pierre gave him a sudden push into his chair. The guard, caught off-balance, sat down heavily and for a moment was too stunned to react.

Jessica grabbed Elizabeth's arm, and they held their hands to their faces to prevent their laughter from exploding. The kids had come to rescue them! Suddenly Jessica was sorry for ever thinking the kids were a bother. How sweet of them to do this!

While the guard struggled and sputtered and shouted French words that the children probably shouldn't be hearing, Claudine danced around the chair with a rope, wrapping it tightly around the guard so he couldn't move. She sang a little song as she skipped. "La, la, la, la . . ."

"I can't believe this," Elizabeth said into Jessica's ear. "They've got him tied up!"

"Les enfants terrible!" the guard screamed until Manon stepped up and shoved a red sock into his mouth. Then he could only moan and glare at them. The kids ignored him. Pierre crouched next to the guard's chair and fiddled with the snap that held the ring of keys to his belt.

"Kids," Elizabeth said, "aren't you going to get into trouble for doing this?"

"Oh, Liz, lay off them, will you? I think it's great what they did. And what do you think their parents are going to do, spank them?" Jessica asked sarcastically. "Would you rather rot in this cell?"

"No," Elizabeth admitted grimly.

Pierre finally got the key ring free, and the kids rushed over to the door. The keys jingled and jangled as Pierre tried first one, then another in the lock. "Where is the key?" he shouted in frustration.

"Let me try," Claudine said, pulling at his arm.

"No!" Pierre shrieked, pulling back. "I will do it!" He returned to trying the keys in the lock one by one while Manon further confused things by jumping up and down and reaching for the keys, crying, "Me! Me!"

Suddenly, with a scrape and a clank, one of the keys turned and the door opened. They were free! The guard just glared at them while Elizabeth hugged Claudine and tried to hug Pierre. Jessica reached down and scooped up Manon in her arms. "You guys are the best!"

After a quick hug Jessica put Manon down and went quickly to check on the guard. Claudine and Pierre had tied the rope tightly, but Jessica gave it one more twist to make sure. "You're not going anywhere for a while," she told the guard with a flippant toss of her head. He glared daggers at her. *Serves him right,* she thought.

Pierre had successfully dodged Elizabeth's embrace and was saying, "Mesdemoiselles Elizabeth, Jessica, you must get away. You must run away from this place. *Alors,* never mind us!"

Jessica knew he was right, but the idea of running away bothered her. It would make them look so guilty. "If we escape, they'll think we were guilty all along," she said to Pierre. "I hate letting the countess gloat over how right she was when she's really totally wrong."

"I know," Elizabeth said glumly. "But who believes us? Even if Prince Laurent stands up for us, he has no way to prove our innocence." She rubbed each wrist painfully and sighed. "The fact is, we were on the train with the countess when the emerald was stolen. And we were in the château when the diamond necklace was stolen. They don't even know that Jacques exists, so they have no other logical suspects."

Jessica scowled, trying desperately to think. Claudine tugged at her arm, and Manon clutched her around the neck.

"I guess you're right," she said finally. "Without Jacques we can't convince anyone of our innocence."

Elizabeth reached out and placed a comforting hand on Jessica's arm.

"Our only choice is to somehow find Jacques, and that means we have to leave," she said in a soothing voice.

"Yes," Pierre agreed, pulling on Elizabeth's hand. "You must to leave."

Elizabeth knelt down in front of the little boy. "Pierre, what you did tonight was very brave. Thank you for freeing us." This time he permitted her to hug him for two seconds before pulling away.

Jessica put Manon on the floor. "I'll never forget you, you little monsters," she said, tears of joy welling in her eyes. She brushed them away impatiently with the back of her hand. "Come on, Liz," she said, heading for the door.

Jessica led the way up the stairs, and they tip-toed along the hallway until they found a door to the outside. Once out in the fresh air they sprinted across the lawn in the direction of the woods.

Elizabeth knew she was more unhappy than Jessica about running away, even though she was sure it was the logical thing to do. All her life she had believed that telling the truth was the only way to go. And for the most part that's what she did, even when the truth was painful or led to her being punished. *But this time it's different,* Elizabeth told herself. *No one will believe the truth until we have proof.*

"Wait, Liz," Jessica said suddenly, pulling Elizabeth's arm to direct her toward a nearby tree. "Where are we going?"

"What?" Elizabeth asked. It was chilly outside, even though it was a summer night. The black sky spread above them, dotted with silver stars, and a breeze gently ruffled the branches of the tree.

"Where are we going? I don't have a clue where Jacques really is. We left all our money back at the château, and we don't know anyone," Jessica said.

"I hadn't thought that far ahead," Elizabeth admitted, leaning against the tree. "It seemed so important just to get out of that cell and find Jacques. We have to figure out where to start."

Suddenly Jessica snapped her fingers. "Jacques must be staying in the town across the river. We can find him if we can just get to town," she said, tossing her blond hair from side to side. "He knows how to get in and out of places without being seen. I know he'll do something to help us, for my sake."

"But Jess, what about the emerald?" Elizabeth asked. "He's the reason we're in this mess in the first place."

"Even more reason for him to help us," Jessica insisted. "Besides, he has some explaining to do about that emerald!"

"But even if he agrees to help us," Elizabeth argued, "I'm sure we can't trust him. There's just something about him. . . ."

Even in the dark Elizabeth could see Jessica's expression change from anxious hope to anger. "All right! If you're so smart, you tell me what we're going to do. What's your big plan?"

With a sinking heart, Elizabeth had to admit the truth. "I don't have a plan," she said quietly. "I guess we don't have any other choice but to try and find Jacques. You're right. He owes us an explanation about the emerald." Elizabeth kept looking around, hoping there were no guards close by. She felt practically naked standing in the darkness outside, wearing a white ball gown. "How far is it to town?" she asked.

"I'm not sure," Jessica admitted. "But if we don't make it tonight, maybe we can flag down a ride in the morning. At least it's some kind of plan."

"OK," Elizabeth said, reluctantly following her twin across the lawn and toward the woods.

○　　　○　　　○

At the café at their inn in the middle of town Jacques and his father were having a late supper. "How is the soup, Papa?" Jacques asked, hoping to divert the older man from his favorite subject: Jacques's shortcomings as a thief.

Louis tasted the aromatic soup gently. "Not bad," he said. "But I have had better."

Jacques let his mind drift from his father's voice while he pushed his food automatically into his mouth. He was more than preoccupied with thoughts of Jessica Wakefield, the beautiful American he had met on the train from Paris. They had talked and joked and flirted the entire first night on the train, and he had known right away that she was someone special.

"Jacques . . . Jacques . . . are you awake?" his father was saying insistently. He tapped Jacques's hand with his finger. "I am asking you what you want to eat. The waiter tells us they have just run out of the beef."

Jacques looked up at the waiter, who was waiting with barely concealed impatience, his foot tapping the flagstone terrace, his pencil poised above his pad. "The veal will do," Jacques said quickly, anxious to be rid of the irritated waiter.

"Where is your head tonight, my boy?" his father demanded. "With that little American?"

Jacques felt himself blush red-hot. "No, of course not, Papa," he mumbled, lowering his eyes to his plate. He pushed the salad greens around a bit. *How can I bear to eat?* he thought. *I can't even taste this food when my mind is so full of Jessica.*

Since that fateful train trip the emerald had become a source of anguish for him and the reason he repeatedly went to see Jessica. He'd had to get it back! His father had promised it to one of their "clients."

But the more time he spent with Jessica, the more she came to mean to him, until his heart leapt at the very sight of her. This only confirmed what he had suspected from the start—he had been falling in love.

As Jacques brought another forkful of green salad to his mouth his father launched into another tirade. "I cannot believe you didn't get the emerald. It's the whole reason you went to the château in the first place," he reminded Jacques. "It was a bad risk, and you came back empty-handed!"

"It's not as if I *intended* to come back without it," Jacques said, trying to be reasonable.

"You should have just snatched it away from her," Louis said between spoonfuls of his steaming soup. "Do you think this is some game we're playing here? You meet an American girl, and you forget everything I have taught you?"

"No, Papa," Jacques responded patiently, wishing his father would speak English so people wouldn't understand his shouting. He hated to fight back when his father got like this, which wasn't often. Of course, this was the first time Jacques had failed to recover one of their jewels. "Things just happened," he finished helplessly.

"Things never 'just happen,'" the older man shot back. "You make things happen. If you don't know that by now . . ." Mr. Landeau threw up his hands. "Jacques, you are my only son . . . my only family. I love you very much," he said in a kinder tone. "And I can understand how a pretty face can turn a young man's head. But you must recover that gem. You know it has to go to our 'friend' as payment for my debt."

"You've explained all that to me before, Papa," Jacques said in a strained voice.

"It doesn't hurt to say it again since your head is in the clouds over a girl." Mr. Landeau sighed, and his blue eyes softened. "Jacques, my Jacques, I don't have anything against that little girl. She's quite pretty. I just want the emerald back." He put down his spoon as a signal he was done with the soup, and the waiter immediately moved toward the table to take the bowl away. "Now, let us not spoil our supper over this matter. You know what you have to do."

"Don't forget, Papa, my visit to the château wasn't a total loss," Jacques pointed out desperately. "I did get the diamond necklace."

"Yes, and it is very nice, Jacques. And it did make up somewhat for your recent bad judgment," Mr. Landeau admitted as he leaned back

27

to allow the waiter to take his soup dish away. "But I think I will not let you work anymore until you get the emerald and until you get over that American girl."

The waiter came back with their main course of tender, perfectly cooked veal and potatoes. Although Jacques's appetite wasn't at its best, he could hardly resist such a delicious meal. As he ate he wondered just what he was going to do about Jessica.

I should never have let myself fall for the girl I had to use to hide the jewel, Jacques silently berated himself. *Will she ever forgive me? How can I ever explain it to her?*

Just as Prince Laurent reached the door of the ballroom a reporter stepped in front of him. *"S'il vous plaît,"* the reporter said insistently as he shoved a microphone into Laurent's face. "Will there be an announcement soon about you and the daughter of the countess?" the man asked in French.

Laurent wanted to roll his eyes in frustration, but there were too many cameras pointed in his direction. "I cannot comment right now," he replied. "Please let me go."

The journalists formed a wall at the door to the ballroom, a seemingly unbreakable barrier. Their eager faces and poised pencils filled Laurent with disgust. *Let me out of here!* he wanted to scream.

Just as he was about to shove them aside he felt a hand on his arm. He turned quickly to see a guard at his elbow. "What do you want?" he asked impatiently.

"Your father wishes to speak with you," the man said in a low, respectful tone.

"Not right now," Laurent said, attempting to shake the man's hand from his arm.

"Your Grace, I'm sorry," the man said. "Your father insists."

Laurent looked at the reporters watching him expectantly, then back at the guard, also waiting for him. He felt like a rat trapped in a cage. There was no way he could openly defy his father to go to the dungeon to see Elizabeth. Besides, the reporters might follow him!

"Very well," he said, defeat freezing his heart. He followed the guard over to the dais where his parents sat.

"Laurent," his father said, standing and pulling Laurent toward a corner of the room in order to achieve some degree of privacy. "I noticed you leaving the ball," he commented sternly.

"Just for a moment, Father," Laurent pleaded. "I'm smothering in this place. It's like being in a fishbowl with the reporters and Antonia."

"Son, do not forget your duty," his father warned. "You may not leave this ball."

"Father," Laurent insisted, placing one hand on his father's arm, "I must see Elizabeth . . . only for a moment."

"That is quite simply out of the question," his father said, his eyes growing wider in agitation.

"It would never do for you to abandon Antonia for the sake of that American girl."

"But she must be terrified in the dungeon," Laurent argued. "I would be there for one moment only, just to reassure her, to let her know that she will soon be released. She will be released soon, won't she, Father?"

The question seemed to make his father uncomfortable. "Now is not the time or place to debate this," he informed Laurent. "My decision stands. You may not leave this ballroom until the evening is over."

Laurent's sense of defeat increased, weighing him down with anguish. "Very well, Father," he agreed, knowing that he couldn't go against his father's wishes so openly. The pain was so intense, his heart actually ached in his chest.

"Laurent, we know this is a difficult situation," his father said. "But you must return to Antonia."

"Yes, Father," Laurent replied woodenly. He squared his shoulders and clenched his fists as he walked toward the corner where Antonia still sat with her terrible mother.

Someday, Laurent thought desperately, *I will do whatever I choose, no matter what anyone says or thinks. And somehow Elizabeth will be with me!*

Chapter 3

"Jessica, we're safe now. I have to catch my breath." Elizabeth bent over and placed her hands on her knees for support. They had just entered the woods, and she felt more secure under the blanket of darkness the trees provided.

"OK, but not for more than a minute," her twin warned.

"Any sign of the guards?" Elizabeth asked, taking in great gulps of the cool night air and resting a hand over her wildly beating heart.

"Not that I can see," Jessica answered, glancing around and squinting into the woods.

They had stopped in a small clearing, surrounded by tall, thick trees. The moon had risen, casting a cool white light over the weeds and shrubs of the small field. The clearing was carpeted in soft grass, which felt spongy beneath

Elizabeth's satin shoes. Crickets sang, and some-where a frog croaked. At any other time Elizabeth would have been soothed by the beauty of the night. But since they'd begun their escape, a con-cern had been weighing on her mind, and she could no longer deny its urgency.

"Jessica," Elizabeth began, "I know we decided that finding Jacques is the right thing to do, and I agree that he owes you an explanation, but . . . I really need to see Laurent. I can't stand the thought of him thinking I'm . . . *we're* thieves . . . and maybe he could help—"

Jessica cut her off with a swipe of her hand through the air. "Elizabeth, the closer we are to the château, the more chance there is that we'll be re-captured. I just don't think it's worth the risk," she finished.

"How would you feel if a guy you really cared about thought you were a criminal?" Elizabeth was close to tears, and in trying to be quiet, her voice came out harsh and raspy.

Jessica nervously raked her hand through her hair. When she spoke, Elizabeth could feel the desperation in her words. "And how are you going to convince Laurent you're not a thief if we end up back in the dungeon?"

Jessica was angry, but Elizabeth wasn't in the mood to go along with her twin. "Jessica Wakefield, you are the one who badgered me into coming to Europe against my better judgment, right?"

"I know, but—"

"And how many times have I gone along with your schemes in the past?" Elizabeth interrupted.

"A few," Jessica mumbled.

"A few? Let's see, there was the time you stayed out all night and I had to cover for you the entire day because you couldn't drag yourself out of bed," Elizabeth began, ticking off her fingers one by one. "And then there was the time at camp when I had to compete in all your color war events . . . need I go on?"

Jessica held up both hands in a classic defensive posture. "OK, OK, I get the point. Enough with the guilt trip!"

But Elizabeth was warming to her subject and refused to let her twin off easy. "You do this to me all the time! You beg and plead until I do what you want, then when we end up in trouble, you're no help at all! Now I want just one little thing, and you have to go all logical on me! How can you let me down like this?"

"Good grief, Liz," Jessica said, grabbing Elizabeth by the shoulders. "Enough already. So we'll go back and try to see Prince Charming. But if we get caught, so help me, Liz . . ."

Elizabeth was exhausted by her tirade, and she gave Jessica a tired smile. "Thanks, Jess."

Jessica let her go and shrugged. "I had to do something to get you to shut up. I bet every guard on the island heard you," she said grumpily. She grabbed Elizabeth by the wrist, and they started back to the château.

As they trudged across the grass Jessica grumbled under her breath, "We came all this way . . . now we have to go all the way back . . . and for some drippy prince. . . ."

Despite their awful situation, Elizabeth was having trouble keeping her laughter in check. "Oh, Jessica," she finally said. "Nag, nag, nag, all the time."

They broke from the woods and approached the château silently. The ballroom was easy to find. Music filtered across the lawn from the partially opened, tall windows that were blazing with light.

With Jessica close behind, Elizabeth crept to one of the windows and peered inside. All the women wore ball gowns, in every color of the rainbow. Precious jewels glittered on each throat and around every wrist. Some of the ladies carried fans, which they flicked back and forth as they floated around the room. The couples who weren't dancing lined the walls, laughing and talking in a carefree manner. Almost everyone was holding a glass of bubbly champagne.

There were so many people whirling around the dance floor, Elizabeth could barely make out their faces. Then a tall, dark-haired guy twirled past, and Elizabeth gasped. It was Laurent. And he was dancing with Antonia . . . and smiling! How could he? Did he care so little for Elizabeth that he could carry on as if she didn't exist?

What I wouldn't give to trade places with that disgusting Antonia! Elizabeth thought desperately. *That should be me in that gorgeous, fairy-tale dress, dancing in Laurent's arms! And Antonia in the dungeon!* She smiled wryly at the thought of Antonia shivering in the cold darkness of that musty cell.

Antonia was wearing a smug look of triumph on her face that made Elizabeth want to scratch her eyes out. She felt a sob catch in her throat at the frustration of it all. A tear rolled down her cheek.

Jessica abruptly pulled Elizabeth away from the window.

Elizabeth whirled around to face her sister. "Oh, Jess, did you see—"

"Forget about the couple of the century for a minute," Jessica interrupted quietly, squeezing Elizabeth's arm reassuringly. "We have company."

Elizabeth's heart froze as she expected to see a troop of guards coming their way.

Instead she saw the three younger children standing behind Jessica.

"What are you three doing out here?" Elizabeth demanded, glad to have something to focus on besides Laurent and Antonia.

Pierre was scowling. "Mademoiselle Elizabeth, why are you still here?"

Jessica rolled her eyes and jerked her thumb at Elizabeth, her mouth twisted into a smirk.

"Lovesick here had to have one last word with your brother," she said sarcastically in a stage whisper.

Pierre leaned over to the giggling Claudine and whispered a flurry of French into her ear. As his younger sister sped off into the château Pierre bowed to Elizabeth with a flourish of his little hand. "I am not as handsome as my brother, but surely, mademoiselle, you have time for one dance with me," he said gallantly, deepening his voice.

"Oh, no," Jessica moaned. "Are you crazy? Now I know we're going to get caught."

"No, pretty Jessica," Pierre said with a smile that was hauntingly like Laurent's. "You are safe. No one even knows you are out of the cell." He held out his arms to Elizabeth, and she couldn't resist the sweet gesture.

Pierre actually danced well, which Elizabeth should have expected. As the son of European royalty, dancing was part of his education. He whirled her around rather expertly.

Jessica threw up her hands. "The whole world is insane," she said, "but who cares? I guess if you can't beat 'em, join 'em." And with that she picked up little Manon and began to dance too.

The music swelled and subsided, swelled and subsided as they glided through the steps of the dance. Manon was seized with fits of giggles, and Elizabeth saw her little hands gripping Jessica in a stranglehold around her neck. Pierre beamed up at her, seeming much older than six. "You dance so well," he said to Elizabeth.

"Thank you, sir," Elizabeth replied primly. "So do you."

"What about us?" Jessica insisted, dipping Manon so close to the ground, she squealed in delight.

"You two look great together," Elizabeth said, laughing. "You know, Jessica, you should dance with more three-year-olds. It suits you!"

"Thanks a lot," Jessica said in her most sarcastic tone.

Elizabeth suspected that Claudine had been sent to get Laurent, and she hoped the little girl would hurry. Just one last word with her prince was all she wanted, then she didn't care what else happened!

Inside the ballroom no one would have guessed that Laurent had his mind on anything but Antonia. He chafed to go to the dungeon for just a glimpse of Elizabeth, but his ever present sense of duty, as well as the unpleasant confrontation earlier with his father, made him stay and see to Antonia's every need.

But this wasn't an easy thing to do, for she needed so much! More champagne, something to eat, another dance, an introduction to a member of the royal family . . . it was endless! It was a struggle not to wince every time she opened her mouth.

They were now moving through a slow dance, and Laurent was stiffly refusing to allow Antonia to press her whole body against his.

"Wasn't it wonderful that the jewel thieves were finally caught?" Antonia asked languidly. "I never rested easy from the moment my mother's heirloom disappeared on the train."

Laurent opened his mouth quickly to respond but then shut it just as fast. He wanted so badly to contradict Antonia. But what was he supposed to say? That he didn't believe the twins were guilty? Based on what? His love for Elizabeth? That would go over well with his fiancée.

"I'm afraid I'm not entirely convinced we have the real thieves," he said quietly. Inside, his heart was aching with longing for Elizabeth, and his mouth went dry every time he thought of her in the dungeon.

Antonia's eyes opened wide, and her lower jaw dropped open in shock. "Laurent, how can you say that?" she insisted. "That horrible, uncultured au pair had the audacity to wear the emerald in public!"

"I have no desire to argue with you, Antonia," Laurent began, straining for patience, "but it hardly seems likely that a thief would display her guilt by wearing the stolen object."

"But Americans are bold and stupid at the same time," Antonia insisted. "I can't believe you're defending them!"

"All I am saying is that no one knows how

Jessica came to have the emerald, and there are many unanswered questions," he said, hoping his firm tone would discourage further comments.

"Well, anyway, they were terrible au pairs, a huge disappointment to your parents." Antonia sniffed, her mouth downturned.

"I cannot speak for my parents," Laurent said stiffly.

"Oh, yes, they ignored the children, they were always late. . . . Americans shouldn't be allowed to take such positions anyway," she stated. "They have such unpleasant notions about equality. Imagine a country with no sense of upper- and lower-class. How gauche!"

Laurent let her voice drift away as he buried himself in his own thoughts. What Antonia had to say was less than important to him. Elizabeth was his only priority. What if she got sick from being locked in that damp old dungeon?

There must be something I can do to help Elizabeth, Laurent thought. *But how can I do anything without hurting my parents and shirking my duty? Why did I have to be born a prince?*

Just then, as Laurent danced Antonia over to the ballroom entrance, one of the journalists took pictures. It reminded Laurent of how publicly he lived his life.

Whenever he rode into town, he watched other boys his age racing to their next class at the university, or walking hand in hand with a girl, or sitting at the café, debating politics with friends. How he envied them!

Tomorrow that picture of Antonia and me dancing will be all over the newspapers, he thought in despair. *Just once I'd like to open my mouth to speak without worrying what words to use or what political position those words put forth. I'd like to go someplace without being followed and photographed!*

"How exciting!" Antonia gushed. She actually stopped dancing and posed beside Laurent, clutching his arm in her hands. She threw back her head and extended one leg to reveal a silver sandal. "How's this?" she asked Laurent.

"Very nice," he said through clenched teeth, hardly able to keep still while the camera flashes blinded him. As soon as the last bulb went off he pressed Antonia to resume the dance so he could blend in with the crowd again.

Laurent's parents smiled at him and Antonia as they glided past the dais. His father was chatting with a foreign ambassador and smiling, but Laurent knew his father disliked the man. *What rubbish!* Laurent thought. *All I want is to be normal, to be free to come and go as I please, to be able to like and dislike whom I will . . . and to be with the girl I love!*

Suddenly he felt a tugging at his coat. He looked down to find Claudine smiling up at him. "What is it, my sweet?" he asked, pulling Antonia away from the stream of dancers and into a secluded corner with Claudine.

Laurent squatted down next to his sister so he was eye to eye with her.

"You must come with me, *mon frère*, now," Claudine whispered in his ear with a secret smile.

Laurent knew instinctively that this had something to do with Elizabeth. He said to Antonia, "There is some emergency with the children, Antonia. Please excuse me for a few moments. I know you will be kind enough to do this."

"Laurent, let me go with you," Antonia whined. "Maybe I can help."

Laurent almost panicked. Was there no way to get her to leave his side? He cast about in his mind for the words to dissuade her. Then a thought came to him, and he had to stop himself from smiling at his ingenuity.

"Antonia, I'm afraid that's not a good idea," he began. "You see, Manon has an upset stomach. I'll spare you the details because you're a lady, but . . . she's made a bit of a mess. The children are afraid to call the servants. If you would like to come along, by all means . . ."

Antonia's long nose wrinkled in distaste. "Perhaps it would be best if you went alone," she said, turning a very faint shade of green.

Laurent heard Claudine giggling behind him as he walked Antonia over to where the countess was standing, talking to friends. Then he followed

Claudine. He didn't even turn around when Antonia's whining voice followed him. "Laurent, when will you be back . . . ?"

This time Laurent muscled his way past the reporters in spite of his father's glare. He was going to see Elizabeth!

For the first time in hours Elizabeth actually felt lighthearted. There was no way to resist Pierre's charm; even at six he reminded her of Laurent, and her heart was touched. *This is real,* she thought. *Everything* else *that's happened—the theft, the accusation, the dungeon—is not part of real life.*

Suddenly she felt a hand on her arm and she spun around, expecting to see a guard.

"Oh," she said, clapping her hand over her mouth.

It was Laurent!

Elizabeth flew into his open arms and laid her cheek against his broad chest. Like magic, nothing mattered anymore. Nothing could really go wrong as long as she was in his arms.

If only I could stay here forever, she thought, nestling deeper into his embrace. She felt his hand reach up to stroke her hair gently. His other arm held her tightly around the waist, as if he would never let her go. *I hope he never* does *let me go,* she told herself.

In the arms of a prince, Elizabeth felt like a

fairy-tale princess. It was like stepping into the picture books she had loved as a child. She felt just as graceful, just as beautiful as the heroines she once adored.

But then Elizabeth couldn't help feeling torn. Laurent was engaged to Antonia—he had to marry her. So no matter how much he said he loved Elizabeth, it didn't mean he would change his mind. She pulled away from him and opened her mouth to explain how she felt, but Laurent put one finger on her lips. "No words, my love," he said softly. "This moment there is you and me and no one else in the world."

Elizabeth desperately wanted to believe him, but Antonia loomed large in her mind. Oh, if only she could just stop thinking about everything! All she wanted was to love Laurent, to let her heart rule instead of her head!

Inside the ballroom the orchestra began a new song. Without a word Laurent began to guide Elizabeth into a waltz. She felt like Cinderella, Sleeping Beauty, and Snow White all rolled into one. She willingly followed her prince into the dance, wanting nothing more than to enjoy this fairy-tale moment of swaying in the arms of a real live prince.

The ballroom windows cast a golden light over the perfectly even flagstones of the terrace as they floated along. Laurent locked Elizabeth's eyes with his own, and her heart overflowed with joy. His hands were warm and strong on her waist and around her hand. Her other hand rested on his broad shoulder.

"I love you so much, Elizabeth," Laurent whispered. "You are the most beautiful girl in the world."

"I love you too, Laurent," Elizabeth replied, warmed at the love she saw in his eyes. "No one has ever made me feel the way you do."

"The thought of you sitting in the dungeon . . . ," Laurent said in a pained voice. Elizabeth saw tears glisten in his eyes.

"I've never stolen anything in my life," she said, desperate to make him believe her. She felt her own tears wet on her cheeks.

"I know that," he assured her, squeezing her a little to punctuate his words. "I wish things could be different. . . . I wish Antonia and I—" He broke off suddenly.

If only Elizabeth could forget everything but Laurent and the waltz. But she couldn't do it. She couldn't take another step and pretend that she wasn't devastated by his engagement. "Laurent, it's no use," she said in despair. "I can't do this, knowing that you and Antonia—"

A shriek suddenly pierced the air. "Thieves!" came the countess's shrill, demanding voice.

Elizabeth gasped as Jessica grabbed her by the arm and said hoarsely, "We have to go . . . *now!*" Images flew by Elizabeth's eyes in a blur: the

44

countess and two guards emerging from the doorway onto the terrace, Laurent's heartbroken face, the prince and the princess following the countess. Then Jessica almost yanked her off her feet.

"Get them!" the countess roared behind her. "Release the hounds!"

Elizabeth followed Jessica down the lawn and toward the woods. Her heart skipped a beat when she heard Laurent calling out to her.

"Elizabeth, please come back!"

Before the guards could get organized, Jessica had dragged Elizabeth halfway across the great lawn. Suddenly it seemed as though the woods were miles away. *So far, so far,* Jessica's heart pounded in time with the rhythm of her feet.

What scared Jessica most of all was the sound of the dogs barking. She could just imagine sharp canine teeth sinking into her leg when they caught up with her and Elizabeth. Would the guards let the dogs tear them limb from limb? Jessica risked a glance over her left shoulder as she madly dashed toward the edge of the forest.

The guards were still on the terrace, holding the dogs' leashes, and no one else seemed to be moving. *Thank goodness,* she told herself, turning back around to concentrate on where she was going. She looked over at Elizabeth, who was running beside her, holding up the skirt of her dress to keep from tripping.

Jessica couldn't believe how romantic it had been when Laurent took Elizabeth into his arms. *Why couldn't that have been me?* she thought with a sudden burst of jealousy. There was no doubt in Jessica's mind that Laurent and Elizabeth felt something really strong for each other. *I thought Jacques and I did too,* she moaned to herself.

She concentrated on the line of trees that loomed ahead.

"Almost there," she gasped to Elizabeth, who nodded and kept running.

Finally they reached the edge of the forest, and Jessica risked another look backward. The guards had moved off the terrace and were following, but they weren't running. *They know we can't get too far away on an island!* she thought.

After what seemed like hours of running, Jessica and Elizabeth were in the woods and surrounded by trees. But instead of going faster, they had to go slower. The ground was covered with leaves and fallen twigs, and roots poked through the soil, forcing them to hike their way carefully through the underbrush. Of course, this also gave them a chance to catch their breath, but Jessica was worried that the guards might be closer to them than she thought.

"The last time . . . I looked back . . . ," she began, her chest heaving from fear as much as from the exertion of their speedy flight, "the guards . . . didn't seem to . . . be hurrying."

"How far . . . can we go?" Elizabeth asked, breathing heavily. "Sooner or later . . . we'll get to the river . . . and it's not like we can swim it. The drawbridge is heavily guarded at night."

"One thing . . . at a time," Jessica huffed.

As Jessica's heart slowed down and she realized that the guards were nowhere near, she could think more clearly. "Liz, what was *with* you back there? I practically had to *tear* you out of Laurent's arms. I've never seen you so hung up on a guy."

Elizabeth sidestepped a fallen branch and picked delicately across some moss with her satin-slippered feet. "I don't know, Jess. Maybe it's being in France and the fact that he's a prince, or maybe it's because he really does love me," Elizabeth offered. "Our connection is so strong, no matter what his parents want him to do."

Jessica ducked under a low branch and tucked a stray lock of hair behind her ear out of the way. "I admit he's handsome and charming, but it looks like his parents are going to win out on this whole engagement thing."

"But he doesn't care a thing about Antonia," Elizabeth said defensively. "Maybe he's just waiting for the right time to tell his parents how he really feels."

"But it looks as if he's willing to go through with it," Jessica continued, "no matter how much he loves you."

"I know it looks that way," Elizabeth said,

desperation in her voice, "but I can't shake the feeling that he's hoping somehow there'll be a way to get out of it."

Jessica couldn't believe how much her twin was counting on Laurent's love for her. "That's just a feeling. And since when do you act only on your feelings?" Jessica had a sudden sense of the world shifting, as though Elizabeth's personality was changing in front of her eyes. What would she do if Elizabeth began to act impulsively? It was an outrageous thought. *Jessica* was the impulsive one!

"I can't ignore how I feel this time," Elizabeth explained. "It's just too strong!"

Jessica stopped for a moment to look around and get her bearings. "Well, Laurent is still a prince, and he will take the throne one day. If you married him, you'd be a princess," Jessica stated. "Do you think you could you handle that?"

"I don't know, Jess. But why are we even talking about this? It's slowing us down," Elizabeth said, fanning her face with her hand. "Never mind about Laurent. Let's just get going. Can you see anyone behind us?"

"No. Maybe we lost them," Jessica said hopefully. "We have to find a way to get to town. The sooner we find Jacques, the sooner we can clear up this mess."

They came to a stream, gurgling between the trees. The sound was somehow strangely comforting in the still of the night. "Now what?" Jessica asked, trying to gauge how far the other side of the stream was.

Elizabeth bent over and stuck her hands in the water, wiping them across her face quickly. "Ooh, that feels good," she said, using the hem of her ball gown to dry it.

Jessica crouched down to do the same. She felt dirty and sweaty. "Well?" she demanded. "Are we going to cross this thing or what?"

"Maybe there are some stepping-stones," Elizabeth suggested, standing and smoothing the front of her ball gown. "Let's look."

They walked upstream a few steps, and Jessica spotted what looked like dry stones sticking up out of the water. "There," she said excitedly, pointing. "Up there it looks like stones. We could try crossing."

"Great, Jess! Let's go," Elizabeth said.

Jessica placed a foot on the first stone, extending her arms to enhance her balance. Then she placed the other foot on the second stone, moved her first foot to the third stone, and half turned to Elizabeth. "This isn't too bad, Liz," she said. "Come on, try it!"

"OK," Elizabeth said tentatively, her foot on the first stone.

"See?" Jessica said. She promptly slid off into the water. "Oh, no! Now on top of everything else my feet are wet!"

"Shhh," warned Elizabeth. "You'll have every

guard on top of us. We can't do anything about your feet right now. You'll just have to live with it."

I hate wet feet! Jessica thought. *But then, hmmm, isn't that what animals do to throw off other animals, walk through water? I can't remember.*

Jessica's thoughts started to spin off in a million directions. *What if we can't find Jacques? And what if he did deliberately steal that emerald? And what if Elizabeth gets all mushy on me again? Oh, why did I ever even think about coming to France?*

Chapter 4

The countess had drawn herself up to her full height and was pacing the prince's study. She had worn white to the ball, and her dress was too formfitting to suit her figure; her jewels too were garish and ostentatious. She turned a hard eye on Laurent and said, "They're nothing but common thieves, young man." The countess leaned her face in much too close to Laurent's, and he could smell her stale breath. "And now they're running away to heaven knows where," she added.

Laurent resisted the impulse to push the countess away from him. His father stood calmly to one side of the massive fireplace while his stepmother reclined in a nearby chair. Their formal attire made them seem more imposing than usual. His father's medals glittered as a sign of military prowess. His stepmother's jewels sparkled in the harsh light of the lamp beside her chair. Their faces were grim.

"I know Elizabeth quite well, Countess," Laurent began quietly. "It's hard to believe that she would steal food if she were starving, let alone a precious gem. There must be some other explanation." He looked at his parents, his eyes pleading for their support.

Laurent's father shook his head, and his voice was firm but sad. "I'm sure your intentions are good, Laurent, but I'm afraid the evidence is rather conclusive," he stated.

The countess huffed, a sound that Laurent couldn't help comparing to a camel's cough. "My dear boy, you are naive, aren't you?" She continued pacing, waving her arms around. "Don't you know anything about American girls? Those two may have sweet faces and pretty blond hair, but underneath they want to get their hooks in you and take you for everything you have."

"Countess . . . ," his stepmother began, but the countess strode up and down the room, ignoring her.

"And by the way," the countess demanded, turning her steely gaze on the prince, "how exactly did they escape? They could not have done it alone. Who helped them?" The countess walked toward Laurent, and he was momentarily afraid she would hit him. "Was it you, perhaps? I saw you trying to leave the ball earlier!"

"Of course not!" Laurent cried in self-defense.

Laurent watched his father close his eyes in fatigue and frustration. "Countess," the older man said in a tired voice, "it was the younger children who somehow managed to disable the guard and free the girls. They are so very young, after all—"

"What?" the countess screamed, cutting off the prince. "Your children have been brainwashed by those horrible girls! What will their punishment be?"

"They are my children, and their punishment is none of your concern," Laurent's stepmother answered coolly. Laurent could tell she was appalled by the countess's audacity and was struggling to stay calm.

"They should be whipped at the very least," the countess continued in her loud tone. "Imagine . . . such behavior . . . such . . ."

Laurent's stepmother rose from her chair and glided toward the countess. She took the countess by the arm and said firmly, "Dear Countess . . . Doloria, you must not tax yourself so." The countess refused to budge and dug her heels into the carpet. "We must return to the ballroom," Laurent's stepmother continued. "Our guests will be wondering where we are."

The countess practically jerked her arm away. "Prince Laurent must be made to understand what went on here earlier, and we must discuss the punishment of the younger children," she insisted. "He must accept the fact that the little American girls are nothing but common thieves! You must assure me the younger ones will be spanked until their bottoms are red!"

The princess turned her back on the countess and crossed the room to the window. Laurent was amazed at her ability to remain composed in the face of such insults.

Laurent's father took the countess's other arm. "But now is not the time for these matters, not when we are expected to entertain our guests," he said stiffly. "Do you want the press to get involved in this matter?"

"Of course I wish to avoid a scandal," the countess conceded with a scowl, "but not at the expense of the truth!"

Laurent, mindful that he was obligated to be polite to this horrid woman, clenched his fists at his sides and said in a tight voice, "I don't care about other American girls. I refuse to believe that Elizabeth did anything wrong." He tried to make his voice softer, gentler. "Please, you must not hunt them down like dogs. Let me find them, and then we can reason through this."

The countess laughed. "An American, reasonable? How absurd, my dear boy. All Americans have the intellects of earthworms!" The countess's voice actually became louder, if that was possible. "No, these foolish girls will be thrown back into the dungeon once they are captured."

The thought of Elizabeth going back to that dank, musty, cold cell made Laurent's stomach turn in disgust. He looked at the three adults—the countess with her hard face, his father looking sad but resigned, his stepmother wringing her hands in distress—and he knew he was on his own. These people would never understand what he knew about Elizabeth, that she was sweet and honest and, above all, innocent.

"Laurent," his stepmother said in an anxious voice, "come back to the ball with us now."

"Yes," the countess interjected in her annoying tone. "Antonia is waiting for you."

Laurent's father tried to put an arm around his shoulders, presumably to herd him back into the ballroom, but Laurent sidestepped the embrace.

"Father, you are so anxious for me to be a man," he said grimly. "But I will never be a man if I do not act now. I'm sorry, but I am going to find the twins."

Laurent knew there was only one thing to do. He would take Pardaillan and ride into those woods to look for the girls. He turned away from his parents and the countess and stalked off in the direction of the stables.

If I can reach the twins before anyone else, Laurent thought as he left the château by a side door, *maybe I can sort through this mess and make everything right. I owe Elizabeth that much at least.*

Pardaillan whinnied at the sound of Laurent's boot steps as he entered the stables. Laurent flung off his constricting uniform jacket and hung it on a nail. He loosened and removed his pure silk tie, which had been feeling more and more like a noose as the evening wore on.

He found his saddle and secured it on the horse. "Easy, boy," Laurent said in French, patting the stallion's hindquarters and pulling the cinch tight around his belly. Laurent next inserted the bit into the horse's mouth, pulled the reins over his head to rest on the saddle, and led him outside before mounting him.

"Yes, Pardaillan," he whispered into the stallion's ear as they turned toward the woods, "you and I are going to find my beautiful Elizabeth and rescue her from the wicked countess." Pardaillan neighed in response as he broke into a gallop.

"I just hope I am not too late," Laurent whispered to the night.

The forest had long ago enclosed the twins in its murky depths. But now the moon had slid behind a dark cloud, leaving them in pitch-darkness. Elizabeth couldn't see where she was putting her feet. It was impossible to tell which was the right way to go. It would be disastrous if they emerged from the woods into the waiting arms of the château guards.

Elizabeth could barely make out the figure of her twin, walking a few steps in front of her. Tree branches clutched at their worn and dirty ball gowns, and Elizabeth wasn't sure how much farther she could go. Her shoulders and legs ached, her arms were covered with scratches from the trees and bushes she had stumbled into, and she thought any moment they would hear the dogs barking.

The darkness was a mixed blessing. If Elizabeth couldn't see, then the guards wouldn't be able to see either. And the soft carpet of moss and leaves on the floor of the forest made it possible for Elizabeth and Jessica to move quietly.

Suddenly Elizabeth's foot sank into a deep hole. She went down hard, her ankle twisting painfully to one side. She let out a little yelp and grabbed at her foot.

"Jess, Jess, stop, I twisted my ankle! Ooh, it hurts!" She sat on the damp grass in her ruined ball gown and rubbed her ankle, trying to ease the pain.

Jessica fell to her knees beside her. "Oh, Liz, what are we going to do?" she cried. "Just when I think it can't get any worse! How could you put your foot in a hole?"

Elizabeth groaned in frustration. "I didn't *see* the hole or I wouldn't have stepped into it," she said tersely.

"You should have been more careful," Jessica accused.

"I didn't do it on *purpose!*" Elizabeth insisted. "Jessica, get a grip!"

Jessica sighed. "I didn't mean to blame you," she admitted, "but this is the worst thing that could happen. How will we ever get out of these woods now, with you like that?" Jessica's voice was near hysterical. "I just don't know how much more I can take!"

"Shhh," Elizabeth said quickly. "Don't get crazy on me now. The guards might be near."

Jessica clapped a hand over her mouth, her eyes wide and scared. "Oh, no," she said in a loud stage whisper. "Now that you can't move, they'll find us for sure."

Elizabeth heaved an enormous groan. "I do know I can't go any farther tonight," she said. "If I could see better, maybe then I might risk it. But if I turn this ankle again, it'll probably break."

Jessica hugged herself tightly, rocking back and forth on her knees. "I'm just so tired. Maybe we should stay here till dawn. Then I can go for help."

"I'm so exhausted, I can hardly keep my eyes open," Elizabeth admitted, "but what if there are wild animals in these woods? There's no way we could defend ourselves. We're like sitting ducks if we aren't on the move."

"But we can't see, and now you can't walk. No, we better stay here." Jessica sounded less shaky. "Don't you remember what the camp director said last summer? Wild animals usually go after food, and we don't have any."

"Oh." Elizabeth groaned. "Did you have to mention food? My stomach is growling."

Just then the moon slipped out from behind a cloud and showered a silvery light between the trees. "Yes!" Jessica said excitedly. "Now that I can see better, I'll try to build us some kind of shelter for the night with these fallen branches. What do you think?"

Elizabeth was heartened by the optimism in Jessica's voice and her boundless energy as she started gathering the branches. "You know, Jess, sometimes you drive me crazy, and you did get us into this mess, but I am awfully glad we're sisters," she said warmly.

Jessica laughed. "Thanks, I'm glad I'm not all that bad." She pulled several branches toward an opening between two sturdy tree trunks.

"That's a good spot," Elizabeth said, trying to shift into a more comfortable position. As she watched her sister lean branch after branch against the trees she couldn't help being impressed. "That looks great, Jess."

"What else did you expect from your perfect twin?" Jessica asked with her nose in the air.

"And modest too," Elizabeth quipped.

Jessica laughed in response. "Now I just have to make the bed. . . ."

"Make the bed?" Elizabeth asked doubtfully.

Jessica laughed again as she began to remove rocks and twigs from the area inside the shelter. When she had cleared a space, she stood up and wiped her hands on her tattered dress.

"There, it may not be our clean sheets and feather pillows from home, but it's a safe place to sleep tonight," she said proudly.

"What a day!" Elizabeth sighed, struggling toward the shelter. "I can't ever remember being this tired."

"Here, let me help you." Jessica supported Elizabeth as she crawled into the shelter, then followed her inside. They draped their sad, dirty ball gowns over exposed skin as best they could and snuggled close together for warmth.

Elizabeth closed her eyes and tried to relax.

Maybe I'll wake up back in my bed in Sweet Valley, she thought. *Maybe this really is just a nightmare.*

Jacques knew it was very late, and he was more than ready to sleep after the argument with his father earlier in the evening. But there was an uneasiness in his stomach, a feeling that something terrible was happening somewhere.

He went to the window of his room, pulled back the blue damask curtain, and peered outside. The street was silent and empty. He turned back into his chamber and sat heavily on the neatly made mahogany bed. *What's wrong?*

he wondered. He was answered by another flutter in his stomach.

Jessica! he realized suddenly. *I just know she's in trouble. Somewhere out there, she's in danger.*

But how could he help? His feelings for Jessica were confusing and strong—he wanted to charm her in the easy, carefree French manner he'd learned from his father, but he also wanted to hold her close and promise his undying devotion. Now that was a joke! Someone who lived the way he did, moving around, never putting down roots, couldn't promise undying *friendship*, let alone devotion!

"What spell have you cast on me, Jessica Wakefield?" he asked the empty room, feeling more like a caged animal every minute.

I have to do something. But what? he thought. *Should I try to find her, try to save her from . . . whatever? Or should I just mind my own business and forget about her?*

"She was better off before I came along anyway," he said aloud.

No, if I have charmed Jessica in this short time since we met, then she has charmed me twice as much. I can't just erase her from my mind. He raked his hand through his hair.

"Perhaps if I return to the château, I can find out what is going on. Maybe there is nothing to worry about," he told the bedside lamp. "And I did see a stable down the street that isn't heavily guarded. I'll bet no one would even miss a horse if I 'borrowed' it for a few hours."

Jacques crept out into the night, feeling energized by his decision to act. He stopped just outside the inn to take stock of the town. Only a cat stirred, stalking among the bushes and small trees.

He slipped down the alleyways in his usual stealthy manner, stopping every few steps to make sure no one had detected him. The stable lock was simple to open, the horses too sleepy to be alarmed.

He chose an average-size horse, dark in color so it would blend with the night. Although Jacques worried about being caught and his sense of fear for Jessica hadn't diminished, he didn't move too quickly. He had learned from experience that the faster you tried to do something covert, the more likely it would go wrong.

Not bothering with a saddle, Jacques secured only the bridle on the horse.

"Come on, old girl," he whispered as he pulled on the reins and led the horse from the stable. Once outside, he walked the horse to the nearby mounting block and swung onto her back. Gripping the horse with his thighs, he pulled the reins to the right, aiming for the road out of town.

Of course, he thought as the horse began to move, *if I return to the château, it might be possible to recover the emerald after saving Jessica from whatever danger she's in. And if I do save her, she'll probably be so grateful, she'll part with the emerald without a whimper. Even though I wouldn't mind tussling for it like we did earlier.* He grinned.

At the edge of town another rider on a large white horse came galloping toward him. As they neared each other Jacques recognized Prince Laurent. *What is that pampered young man doing so far from his glittering château? And at this time of night!*

"Hmmm," Jacques said to himself, "I wonder how much money he carries?" Then he rolled his eyes at his own thieving reflex and mentally slapped himself. "I'm supposed to be changing!"

Aha, he suddenly remembered, *Jessica mentioned that her sister had attracted the attention of the prince himself. Perhaps he is doing the same thing I am . . . trying to find the twins. So they are in danger! They must have left the château for the prince to come all this way so late at night. Maybe if I stop to talk with him, I will learn something useful.*

Laurent almost slipped from the saddle in exhaustion when he reached the edge of the town. He felt as if he'd combed every inch of the forest. Now, as a last resort, he was going to look in town. It was just possible that Jessica and Elizabeth had made it this far.

The town was as still as a tomb. Not even a cricket dared to disturb the night's quiet. Pardaillan's hooves sounded unusually sharp and loud as they struck the cobbled streets. Laurent's tired eyes scanned the road even as his brain registered the fact that there was no one to see. *What will I do if they aren't here?* he wondered. *What if I can't find them?*

Then he noticed a young man riding toward him. Laurent reined in Pardaillan and tried to smile. "A bit late for a ride, isn't it?" he called to the rider in French.

"Or early. I could say the same for you, Your Grace." Atop his horse the young man bowed with a flourish of his hand.

"So you know me," Laurent said. "Have we met before?"

"I do not believe so," the young man answered easily. "I know you only from reputation. I am but a poor farmer and have not had the opportunity to mingle with royalty. Until now, of course." A casual smile lit his face.

Laurent bristled at another reminder of his removed social position. There was no reason he shouldn't socialize with such a polite and friendly man.

"Well, I'm glad we've had the opportunity to meet, Mr. . . ." Laurent raised an eyebrow in question.

"Pardon me, Your Grace. I am Jacques Landeau." The young man bowed again briefly.

"It is a pleasure to meet you, Monsieur Landeau," Laurent said, nodding. "Unfortunately I must be going. I hope you will pardon my rudeness."

"But if you will pardon *my* presumption, Your Grace, you appear to be distracted and hurried," he said. "Is there some way I can be of service to you?"

Laurent had never felt so frantic in his life, but he had also never felt so tired. *I have never had a friend to confide in,* he thought, *but I am so full of thoughts and feelings.* And when he looked up, young Jacques Landeau was still giving him that quizzical expression. Did Laurent dare take this stranger into his confidence?

"First I must ask," he said quickly, "are you a journalist? A member of the press?"

"Hardly," Jacques said with a laugh. "I am a farmer, as I told you. If there is anything I can do . . ."

Laurent considered his offer again, considered whether he trusted this young stranger enough to confide in him. It was clear he was getting nowhere by himself. Another pair of eyes and ears would no doubt help the search. He quickly decided that it was worth the risk.

"Two young American girls came to the château this summer as au pairs for my younger brother and sisters," Laurent explained. "The countess who is visiting us has had two pieces of valuable jewelry stolen recently, and one of them was found in the possession of one of the American au pairs."

Laurent knew he sounded hysterical, but he was too tired to care. He wasn't even sure this young man could help, but just putting his fears and thoughts into words made him feel immeasurably better.

"The girls were thrown into the dungeon," he continued, "but somehow they escaped, and I have been searching the woods for them. All night, in fact." He pulled on the reins to steady the agitated Pardaillan, and Jacques's horse sidestepped in response.

In the uncertain light of near dawn Laurent thought Jacques had turned a shade paler, and his eyes seemed to widen slightly.

"There were two American girls on the train when I traveled here," Jacques said. "Let me see, can I remember their names? Blond, very pretty . . ."

Was Laurent imagining the quaver in Jacques's voice? "Their names are Jessica and Elizabeth Wakefield."

Jacques's hand clenched on the reins, and Laurent noticed his thighs tighten around the horse's sides. "I believe Jessica and I spoke briefly on the train," Jacques said slowly. "How can you be sure they did not steal the gem?"

"I have come to know one of them . . . Elizabeth . . . extremely well," Laurent explained. "It is inconceivable to me that she would steal anything. But since the girls are only au pairs and

Americans, no one wants to believe in their innocence."

"And you say they have escaped? Then the guards are after them," Jacques said, turning still paler. "They must be terrified."

"Yes, I am sure they are," Laurent agreed. "That's why I need to find them. I'm sure I can straighten everything out. There must be a logical explanation for Jessica wearing that stolen emerald." He ran a hand over his eyes, which felt as if an entire beach full of sand had taken up residence there.

Dawn was only moments away. Laurent looked up at Jacques and thought, *There is something unusual about this young man and his reaction to my story. He seems much more agitated than a true stranger would be. Is it possible he talked to Jessica for more than a few moments? All the more reason for him to help!*

"If you are willing to help," Laurent began, "I would be very grateful. Two heads are better than one, as the saying goes."

Jacques felt like he was falling over a cliff. *Oh, no! How could this happen? I can't believe I caused Jessica and her sister to be accused of this theft. What am I going to do to help them?*

"Of course I will help you, Your Excellency," Jacques said, trying to stay composed.

"Thank you, my friend. And please call me

Laurent. I hate titles," the prince said, steadying his horse by patting the big stallion's neck and cooing softly. Jacques was surprised by the prince's gesture of familiarity. Maybe royalty wasn't all bad.

"Now that we are a team, what should our first move be?" Laurent asked. Obviously the prince had begun to think of Jacques as an ally, and Jacques decided to encourage that.

"You said you have been searching all night, so you must be very tired," Jacques said. "Return to the château to rest, and I will take over the search." He looked at his watch, which he could now read in the growing dawn light. "I will contact you in three hours whether I find them or not, agreed?"

"I would feel much better if I could come with you. I believe they are still in the woods," Laurent said, stretching upright as if to ease his aching back. "We could each enter from a different side and meet in the middle, fan out from there."

Jacques couldn't permit Laurent to accompany him. If he did find the girls, they would be sure to ask dangerous questions about the emerald and his involvement in the crime. But he also couldn't afford to make the other young man suspicious.

"You look ready to drop from the saddle," he observed. "What would your father and mother do if something happened to you, if you fell asleep and then fell off your horse?"

"It is imperative that I continue searching with

you," Laurent insisted. "With both of us out here it greatly increases our chances of finding them."

Jacques could feel his hands turn clammy on the reins. So the parental concern tack wasn't going to work.

"They might not have continued through the woods," he suggested. "What if they doubled back to the château?"

Laurent's eyes widened in astonishment and understanding. "You are right!" he cried. "They might be there even at this moment, and if I am not present, my parents will surely throw them in the dungeon again!"

"Without a doubt," Jacques agreed eagerly. "With you back at the château and me searching out here, we have both places covered." Jacques sighed in relief. He was on his own again, just the way he liked it. "Three hours and I will call," he told the prince.

"Three hours," Laurent cried as he wheeled his magnificent stallion around and started off in the direction of the château.

Jacques turned his own horse toward the woods, watching Laurent grow smaller and smaller as he galloped away. All the while his mind raced.

My dear, sweet Jessica! First trapped in a dungeon and now desperately fleeing through the woods to escape. And it was cold last night! She might be sick or hurt somewhere in those woods! And all because of me.

Jacques groaned out loud at this new twist. He wanted more than ever to change. He and his father had lived this life of crime for too long, and his father's failing health made it even more necessary for them both to reform their ways. Once he found Jessica and somehow made everything right, he would do whatever it took to make his father give up on crime.

Resolutely Jacques spurred the horse forward and into the woods. *Just hold on a while longer, Jessica,* he pleaded silently. *I'm coming for you.*

Chapter 5

Dawn was tingeing the sky pink when Jessica first opened her eyes. She heard a groan and rolled over to look at Elizabeth.

"Oh, my ankle!" Elizabeth cried with a wince.

"Let me see," Jessica said. She sat up and pushed aside Elizabeth's now filthy white ball gown. The ankle that she had twisted the night before was swollen and ugly red in color. "It looks pretty bad."

"What are we going to do?" Elizabeth asked in what was for her an unusually whiny voice. "I can't walk on this ankle."

Although on the inside Jessica felt like a scared little girl, it wouldn't help either of them if she acted like one. She bit her lip, trying to think what to do.

"Maybe you should stay here and I should go find help," Jessica suggested.

"Great. Just leave me stranded," Elizabeth answered, shifting her position so there was no weight on her ankle.

"Well, what do you want me to do?" Jessica wailed. "How far do you think we can get if I have to support you on my shoulder?"

"I don't know, Jess. But I really think we should stick together. I mean, you can barely speak French. How are you going get help if you can't explain the situation?"

I hate this! Jessica thought. But she had to admit that Elizabeth was right. She wasn't going to get very far on her limited vocabulary.

"So we'll find Jacques in town, like we originally decided," she said in resignation. "We'll just have to go as fast as we can without getting you hurt again. Let's see what I can do about making something for you to lean on."

"That's silly, Jess," Elizabeth said in the same whiny voice, which was beginning to get on Jessica's nerves. "What are you going to use around here to make a crutch?"

"Just you wait and see," Jessica said, still trying to be cheerful. Under her ball gown she was wearing a long slip that would be perfect for binding branches together. She took it off and ripped it into several long strips of material. Then she gathered three thick branches and ripped the smaller twigs off each one.

"What are you doing?" Elizabeth asked, trying

to massage the pain out of her ankle.

"Making something to help you walk, silly," Jessica said firmly.

"Since when did you turn into such a Boy Scout?" Elizabeth asked, sounding slightly amused.

"Never mind," Jessica shot back. Using the strips of her slip, she bound the thick branches together as tightly as she could. She found some soft moss at the base of a tree and bound this to the top with the last strip of material. It was a crude crutch, but it might work. "There," Jessica announced. "How's that for imagination?"

Elizabeth rolled her eyes. "Not bad. Should I applaud?"

"Of course," Jessica said with a toss of her head. "And any donations will be gratefully accepted."

"Come on," Elizabeth grumbled. "Let's find Jacques and get this thing straightened out so I can take a bath and change clothes. I feel totally grungy!"

"Me too," Jessica agreed.

Elizabeth rolled over on the ground to her hands and knees. Then she carefully put her good foot flat. Using a nearby stump for leverage, she managed to stand up. "OK," she said, "here we go!" Holding up her hurt foot, she reached for the crutch, and Jessica handed it to her.

"That's it, Liz," Jessica said encouragingly while Elizabeth positioned the crutch beneath one arm. Then she gripped the crude instrument at its midpoint, moved it forward about a foot, and leaned on it while she swung her good foot forward and onto the ground.

Jessica jumped up and down and clapped. "That's great! It really works!" she cried.

"It might be slow going," Elizabeth warned. "But at least we can get to town sometime today."

"I hope the guards have given up by now. There's no way I could run at this point," Elizabeth commented as she and Jessica began wandering through the woods again.

"We're almost to the town, and we haven't seen any guards since last night, so don't worry about it," Jessica said reassuringly.

Just after dawn they crossed the drawbridge over the river that separated the chateau's land from the town.

"Only a little farther to go!" Elizabeth said, feeling better now that she could see the roofs of the town buildings in the distance.

"I'm so tired and hungry," Jessica moaned when they finally reached the edge of town.

"Try not to think about it," Elizabeth said grimly, holding the edge of her skirt above the ground with one hand while using the makeshift crutch as best she could with the other.

"But I can't even remember the last time we ate," Jessica went on. "And look how disgusting these dresses are!"

"They are pretty bad," Elizabeth admitted, looking down at what was once a beautiful, white, fairy-tale ball gown. It was now just a tattered, dirty rag, and it made her feel filthy. "But we can't do anything about that now. Let's just find Jacques."

"Jacques," Jessica said through clenched teeth. "When I get my hands on him . . ."

"Don't put all the blame on him, Jess," Elizabeth said. "You should have never trusted a stranger in the first place."

Jessica stopped dead in her tracks, and her eyes opened wide. "Well, is that the thanks I get for taking care of you last night?" she asked incredulously. "Building someplace for us to sleep and then making a crutch so you could walk? Hmph!" She turned her back on Elizabeth and folded her arms.

Elizabeth felt suddenly deflated. "I'm sorry, Jess," she conceded. "The last thing we should do is fight with each other. We have enough trouble on our hands."

Jessica turned slowly, and Elizabeth noticed tears in her eyes.

"Apology accepted," she said with a pout. "And don't yell at me anymore. I'm just as upset about this as you are!"

"OK, OK. Anyway, you know I can't stay mad at you for long. Let's go," Elizabeth said, trying to smile.

They limped into town, and Elizabeth tensed, expecting a legion of guards to attack them at any moment. Luckily the coast was clear.

"You have no idea where Jacques is staying?" Elizabeth asked.

"I don't remember the name of the place. In fact, I can't remember whether he even told me or not," Jessica said thoughtfully, chewing on her lower lip. "But how many hotels can there be? Look, you can see the end of the town from here."

The first inn was a quaint building designed like a French château. There was a café with sidewalk tables arranged outside and balconies on each window, which must have given the rooms a great view. For a fleeting moment Elizabeth wished she were a guest here so she could crawl upstairs and right into a nice bubble bath. She followed Jessica inside and found the innkeeper, a short, stout woman in a flowered dress and white apron.

"Do you have a Jacques Landeau staying here?" Jessica asked in English.

The innkeeper just shook her head. "Oh, well, Liz, let's go. . . ."

"Wait," Elizabeth said. She turned to the innkeeper and said in French, "Did you understand? We are looking for a young man named Jacques Landeau. He might be staying here with his father, the duke of Norveaux."

"There is no Landeau registered here," the innkeeper said gruffly in French. Then she laughed roughly. "And who is the duke of Norveaux? There is no such person!"

"Are you sure?" Elizabeth asked, trying to keep the desperation from her voice. She was so tired and hungry, and it felt like they would have to walk miles just to get to the next inn.

The innkeeper shook her head. "Even when you speak our language, you refuse to understand," she told Elizabeth in French. "Look at you in your dirty rags, trying to find a person I've never heard of. Norveaux?" She laughed again. "There is no such place!"

"Now what are we going to do?" Jessica moaned.

Elizabeth took a deep breath. "We can't give up yet," she said hopefully. "There's more than one inn, right? So let's go to the next one."

"Are you sure you can walk, Liz?" Jessica asked, her brow creasing into a frown. "Wouldn't you rather sit here while I check?"

"I'm not letting you out of my sight," Elizabeth warned. "What if the guards got you?"

"They wouldn't get me without a fight," Jessica assured her.

"Heaven help them," Elizabeth said ruefully. "Never mind. We go together or not at all."

"All for one and one for all?" Jessica teased.

"You got it," Elizabeth said, really smiling for the

first time. But inside she was worried. *What if Jacques has left town? How will we ever get out of this mess if he's disappeared?* she wondered to herself.

Jessica turned toward the door and smacked into the person coming in. Elizabeth looked up and gasped.

"Jacques!" she and Jessica both said at the same time.

"Jessica, you're safe!" Jacques cried as he grabbed Jessica by the shoulders and practically lifted her off the ground in a hug. His handsome face reflected both relief and exhaustion. "I can't believe it!" he cried.

Jessica was struggling in his arms. "Let me go, you creep!" she screamed. He immediately obliged, taking a step back.

Jacques's shoulders visibly slumped, as though he had suddenly taken on a heavy burden.

"I'm sorry," he said in a tired voice. "I was just so worried about you." There were dark circles under his eyes, and his mouth was down turned and sad. He looked as though he'd been up all night.

Elizabeth looked at Jacques, then at Jessica, whose feelings were written all over her face. Obviously Jessica still cared about Jacques, but she also looked suspicious.

"Where have you been?" Jessica demanded.

"I've been looking for you," he replied. "I ran into Prince Laurent last night. . . ."

"So you know?" Elizabeth asked harshly. "You

know about all the horror we've endured? How could you do this to us?"

"Please, please . . . ," Jacques said, his hands outstretched. He tried to touch Jessica's arm, but she flung him off.

"I want answers," Jessica began sternly, "and I want them now. Where did you get that emerald?" Jacques firmly took her arm and tried to lead her to a chair in the corner, but Jessica jerked away again.

"Don't touch me!" she said, but her expression softened.

Elizabeth noticed that the innkeeper and another bystander were watching them. "Shhh," she said, "let's not make a scene. Jacques, are you staying at this inn? The innkeeper kept telling us she never heard of you."

Jacques's face turned red. "Um, um . . . ," he said.

"The *truth*, Jacques," Jessica insisted, "if you can figure out how to tell the truth!"

Jacques squared his broad shoulders and said firmly, "My father and I are staying here, but we are not registered under the name Landeau. Jessica, Elizabeth, there is a lot you don't know about me. I'm sorry I tried to deceive you, but my name is not Landeau and I am not a duke's son."

Jessica sucked in her breath sharply and clapped a hand over her mouth. She groped backward, and

Elizabeth grabbed her arm and awkwardly led her to the big, overstuffed chair in front of the lobby fireplace.

"I can't stand it . . . ," Jessica said from behind her hand. "I believed in you!"

Elizabeth's heart went out to her sister as she watched the cold reality of Jacques's words register on Jessica's face.

Jacques swallowed hard. "Please, you must allow me to explain," he said in a shaky voice. "At least hear what I have to say."

Jessica was crying now, the tears making wet tracks down her cheeks. "How could you?" she said over and over. "How could you do this to me?"

Elizabeth wiped one hand across her eyes, struggling not to collapse with fatigue. "Jacques, can you tell us the truth?" she asked. "Will it be the truth? Because we're in a lot of trouble. . . ."

"I know," he said resignedly. "And I want to help."

"All right," Elizabeth said, making the decision for both herself and her sister. Jessica didn't look capable of doing much of anything. "We'll listen."

Laurent tossed and turned for two hours, then gave up trying to sleep. He had never heard from the young man, Jacques Landeau, and he thought that was an ominous sign. Could he still be searching?

He went for a walk in the early morning,

trying to exorcise the demons of the night, but it was no use. He could think of nothing but Elizabeth, lost somewhere, cold and alone. Even the sight of the pond didn't soothe him as it usually did. Instead it brought back memories of the happy times they'd spent there. *Where are you, Elizabeth?* Laurent thought as he gazed into the still blue water.

While he was heading back to the château, contemplating whether or not to start the search again, a guard approached. He handed Laurent a written summons to his parents' private drawing room, where they received close friends and family in a less formal atmosphere. Laurent dreaded this meeting, for he knew they would talk about Elizabeth's alleged crime. He knew the twins' escape didn't look good, but his heart told him Elizabeth was innocent. He somehow had to make his parents understand.

His hands were clammy and his shoulders were tense when he entered the private drawing room. His father was pacing up and down on the elegant Oriental rug before the fireplace, and his stepmother sat on the couch.

At least they looked less threatening than they had the night before. His father wore a simple dark blue business suit, with a crisp-looking immaculate white shirt and maroon silk tie into which he had poked a diamond tie tack. His stepmother had on a beautiful yellow silk dress that flowed around her ankles.

Neither one of them smiled, but at least his stepmother had a look of compassion on her face.

"Good morning, Father, Stepmother," Laurent began.

The prince stopped pacing and looked Laurent up and down. "The au pairs," he began, "are obviously guilty, my son. Why else would they have run away last night? Can you tell me that?"

He stopped, apparently to give Laurent a chance to answer his question, but Laurent said nothing.

"It appears the countess is right about the American girls," the older man went on. "They are nothing but common thieves!" His voice was stern and a frown cut deep into his forehead as he resumed his pacing and stopped once to shuffle some papers on his desk.

Laurent's stepmother delicately cleared her throat. "We understand how you feel, Laurent, how much you wish the countess to be wrong."

"Don't coddle him!" the prince warned as his anger obviously increased. "I will not tolerate any more discussion about the supposed innocence of those thieving young Americans. It is most obvious that the countess has been right all along." He wiped a hand over his face. "I should have known better than to trust an American. I have had many business dealings with them and had come to respect them. But I should have remembered they are still foreigners. I risked our children, no less!"

Laurent forced himself to keep quiet, hoping that his silence would somehow calm his father's rage. He had never seen him quite this angry before, and it was a daunting sight. He fought off the temptation to cringe.

"Yes," his stepmother admitted sadly, "I had grave reservations about the girls even before I met them. Do you remember, my dear?" she asked his father.

"Yes, yes," his father replied. "The age was the thing. Sixteen is quite young to take on such responsibility." He shook his head in dismay.

"That's why we hired both of them rather than one, because of their youth," his stepmother said. "Now I see our mistake. They are too young to be responsible."

Laurent's father nodded. "Yes, dear, you were right all along, it seems. You were wiser than I." He punctuated his remark by flinging both hands up in the air in a gesture of frustration.

Finally it seemed as if Laurent's silence made an impression on his father, for the older man stopped pacing and approached him. Face-to-face with his father, Laurent resisted the urge to lower his eyes.

"Laurent, what have you to say for yourself?" the prince demanded.

"I will never believe that Elizabeth stole that emerald," he began firmly. "She hasn't a dishonest bone in her body."

His father rolled his eyes, but his stepmother

spoke from her seat near the window, more coolly this time.

"It is obvious to us that you have become . . . *attached* to Elizabeth, but the jewel was found in her sister's possession," she insisted. "Surely you have some explanation for that if you are so certain Elizabeth is innocent."

Laurent hung his head and said quietly, "I have no explanation." Laurent would hate himself forever for his next words, knowing how badly they would hurt Elizabeth if she heard them. He knew Jessica meant more to Elizabeth than just about anyone else in the world.

"But please remember, the jewel was found in *Jessica's* possession, not Elizabeth's," he said, immediately feeling guilty. "You can't blame Elizabeth for something Jessica may have done." He fervently hoped Elizabeth would never find out how disloyal he had been.

Now, for the first time, his stepmother was openly and clearly unsympathetic. She sat up straighter in her seat, and her fingers drummed restlessly on the table beside the couch.

"You can't honestly believe Elizabeth would not know," she insisted. "They're right next to each other in those tower rooms. How could she not know her twin sister had something so obviously valuable?" she asked.

"But we never even heard their explanation," Laurent insisted, walking up and down a few steps to relieve his frustration. *How can I get through to them?* he wondered helplessly. "They were just thrown into the dungeon without the opportunity to speak."

His stepmother waved one hand dismissively. "There was no time for them to speak. There was the ball to see to, and we could not afford any negative publicity on such a public occasion," she explained.

His father raked one hand through his hair. "You must learn, Laurent, that scandal is the one thing royalty must avoid." The older man went to his desk, where his pipe rested in an ashtray. He went about the business of filling and lighting his pipe, using tobacco that he carried in a breast pocket and a solid gold lighter from the desktop. Soon the air was filled with the aroma of pipe smoke. Laurent had always found the smell curiously comforting.

"I admit we might have handled it differently," his stepmother continued, "but it's done now. And we would have let them out of the dungeon to explain first thing this morning." She used her right hand to adjust the diamond tennis bracelet on her left wrist. "Unfortunately the fact that they ran away does complicate matters."

"We cannot ignore that fact," his father interjected, brushing some imagined dust off the cuff of his suit jacket and puffing on his pipe. "Nor can we ignore the importance of the countess, who suffered the loss. Do you realize how unpleasant she could make things for all of us?"

The thought of the countess wielding her power against them must have ignited his father's anger once again because he resumed his pacing.

"This is an international incident already! And the countess has threatened to call a press conference and *publicly* accuse the girls if they aren't found soon!" he shouted, pounding on a nearby desktop to punctuate his words.

"Yes, Laurent." His stepmother picked up where his father left off. "And you know how difficult it is to appease the countess. I'm worn out trying to keep her occupied, let alone cope with this situation."

Laurent was dizzy from the constant barrage, though he realized all that his parents said was true. But he just couldn't give up.

"Then at least allow me to find them myself," he pleaded. "They must be terrified, with the dungeon and the dogs and all. Elizabeth will trust me, and then we might get to the real truth."

Laurent's father cleared his throat. "And what about the missing diamond necklace?" he asked more quietly. "That was stolen right here in the château."

Laurent's stomach clenched. "I don't know. But my heart tells me the twins did not steal anything. . . . They are not criminals . . . at least not Elizabeth. I am willing to do whatever it takes to help prove that."

Laurent's father stroked his cheek thoughtfully, apparently considering his son's words. He strolled over to the window to look outside, and for a long time Laurent wondered if he would say anything at all. The smoke from the pipe curled upward from the window in a lazy ribbon.

"All right," he said finally, "I will make a deal with you. I wish to secure our country's future by your marriage to Antonia di Rimini. But it has become obvious to me that you do not wish to marry her." He turned from the window with raised eyebrows, and Laurent nodded uncertainly. "If I can promise that the countess will not prosecute the girls, will you fulfill your duty? Will you marry Antonia?"

Laurent felt as if his father had reached inside him and torn out his heart. He reached for something, anything to lean on, and when he realized there was a chair nearby, he sat down quickly. His knees had turned to jelly, and his head was swimming.

Is this man really my father? he wondered to himself. *How can he suggest such a thing? How can he ask me to make that choice? Doesn't he realize he's making me throw my life away?*

"I don't know what to say, Father," he began, his voice sounding hollow in his ears.

His stepmother stood up and joined the elder prince. She refused to meet Laurent's eyes, and he could see the reddish tinge of a blush in her cheeks.

"I must see to the countess, my dear," she said to his father. "I'm sure I can smooth her ruffled feathers for the time being, until you bring her Laurent's decision." She left the room.

Finally Laurent looked up at his father, who was still standing beside the fireplace. His father's expression was stern and unyielding, and for the first time in his life Laurent came close to disliking his own father.

"How can you be sure the countess will agree to drop the charges against the twins?" he began, desperately hoping there was some other way to help Elizabeth.

"This political alliance means as much to the countess as it does to us," he said in a slow, deliberate manner. "If I can assure her that you will marry Antonia, I'm more than certain she will agree to my terms." The older man reached up to smooth the front of his tie.

Laurent knew his father was right. Even the countess was intelligent enough to have noticed that Laurent was less than interested in Antonia. Letting a couple of teenage girls go back to America with a clean record would probably be trivial compared to risking an international incident. Laurent lowered his head and stared at his clasped hands in his lap.

"Please make up your mind, Laurent," his father persisted. "Agree to this marriage, and Elizabeth is free."

Laurent took a deep breath. He felt trapped, and all he wanted was to run from the château and never look back. There must be someplace in the world where he wouldn't have to face this hopeless decision! His father might as well throw him into the dungeon. Marriage to Antonia would be like prison. *Worse.*

And yet Laurent's heart constricted as he realized he was Elizabeth's only chance. How much did he love her? Enough to throw his life away for her sake? And if he didn't marry Antonia, would he be able to live with what would happen to Elizabeth? There was really only one choice, wasn't there?

"Very well, Father," he said softly. He pressed the palms of his hands down hard on his thighs to keep them from shaking. "I will marry Antonia."

The prince smiled for the first time since Laurent had entered the room. "That's my boy," he said, his relief obvious as he approached Laurent and patted him on the back. "I knew you would do the right thing in the end, son."

Laurent wanted to fling his father's hand away, but he did nothing. He had promised to live a life of misery. A life devoid of love and passion. *But it was surely worth it,* he thought with grim determination. He would do anything in his power to save the only girl he would ever love—Elizabeth Wakefield.

Chapter 6

Once Jessica and her sister were safely behind the closed door of Jacques's shabby room, she whirled on him with fury.

"How could you do this to me?" she demanded. "How could you set me up like this?"

She clenched her fists, and her chest heaved with anger. "What kind of creep are you to talk about love while lying through your teeth about who you are? I want answers . . . *now!*" She wanted to scratch his eyes out, or pull his hair, or . . . *something*, anything to make him feel as much pain as she was suffering.

Jacques kept his eyes lowered while Jessica was screaming. His shoulders were slumped, and he kept his hands very still at his sides. When he finally raised his eyes to her, the pain in them made her almost sorry she had yelled so loud . . . *almost*.

"Jessica—" he began.

"Do you realize everything we've been through?" she continued, steeling herself against the sudden wave of pity she felt for him. "We were in the woods all night! In the cold! With no blankets, no coats, nothing to eat!"

"That, at least, I can fix," Jacques said quietly, picking up the phone.

Jessica felt faint at the thought of food. She could tell Elizabeth was feeling the same way, and her heart thawed a bit at Jacques's immediate thoughtfulness. She wished desperately that there was some logical explanation for everything he had done to them. He was so handsome, and they had shared so many special moments. She couldn't help loving him, even after all that had happened.

Minutes after Jacques called down to the kitchen, the innkeeper brought up a tray of flaky croissants, strawberry jam, and a big pot of strong coffee. Jessica and Elizabeth immediately dug in, each grabbing a pastry while Jacques poured the coffee. The simple act of eating released much of the tension in the air.

"How did you run into Prince Laurent last night?" Elizabeth asked, spreading some jam on a croissant.

Jacques offered a steaming cup to Jessica and began filling another one for Elizabeth.

"I felt that Jessica was in danger," he said. "So I

borrowed a horse and rode out of town to try and see you at the château. I met Prince Laurent coming into town, and he told me what happened."

"You felt that I was in danger?" Jessica asked, her heart leaping at the thought of how strong their connection was. Then she noticed the intent stare her twin had fixed on Jacques.

"Prince Laurent was looking for us?" Elizabeth asked with wonder in her voice.

"Yes. In fact, he was quite worried," Jacques said, smiling for the first time. "He told me he did not believe you were thieves."

Elizabeth sighed, and Jessica saw tears come to her eyes. "Even after all that's happened, he still believes in us!" She wiped at her eyes and placed her half-eaten croissant on a plate.

Jacques didn't touch his food, and Jessica noticed his leg bouncing up and down nervously.

"It is time for me to be honest," he began slowly. He looked down at his hands, clasping and unclasping them. "My real name is Jacques Savant."

He studied their faces for their reaction to his words, then lowered his eyes again.

"Uh, hmmm . . . ," he stuttered. "M-My . . . my father and I are commoners . . . and . . . we make our living . . . as jewel thieves." The last three words came in a rush, then he stood up and went quickly to the window.

Jessica could see how difficult this whole thing

was for Jacques, but she was too shocked to care. She dropped the croissant she was holding and jumped to her feet. "You . . . you . . . creep! You knew all along exactly what you were doing. You set me up deliberately, and now Elizabeth and I are going back to that horrid dungeon!" The traumatic events of the past twenty-four hours caught up with Jessica, and she burst into tears.

"I knew you were a fraud," Elizabeth said angrily.

Jacques turned quickly from the window and grabbed Jessica by the arms.

"Please, Jessica, give me a chance!" His face was very pale as he looked deeply into her eyes.

Jessica struggled and tried to break free, but Jacques was too strong. She wriggled for a moment more and then was still. She felt positively overwhelmed by everything that had happened over the past few days.

"They set dogs on us . . . we ran and ran . . . and Liz hurt her ankle!" The words spilled out of her mouth.

"Oh, Jessica," Jacques said, trying to pull her close. "You will never know how sorry I am."

She jerked herself free and pushed him away as hard as she could. He fell back a few steps, and his stricken look told her how much the rejection hurt him.

"Don't touch me! I don't want you near me after what you did to me!" she screamed.

"I said I was sorry, and I do still love you. At least listen to my story," Jacques pleaded.

Jessica calmed somewhat at the soft, firm strength she heard in his voice. The plea in his warm brown eyes was nearly irresistible, and she sat down next to Elizabeth.

"Well?" she demanded, determined not to make this easy on him.

"When I was very young," Jacques began, taking a seat across from Jessica, "my mother and father and I lived in Paris. My father sold vegetables, and my mother was a seamstress for many rich people." Jacques's eyes turned wistful at the memory.

"Her work was so good, many of them would consult no one else for their fancy ball dresses and suits for afternoon tea. But then," he said, pain turning his voice harsh, "*Maman* got sick, and my father went to her rich clients, convinced that because of her service to them they would willingly help with the expensive medicine she needed."

Jacques sucked in his breath, and Jessica felt her eyes start to fill with tears all over again. He looked so distraught and helpless. She couldn't believe the effect he had on her.

"What happened when your father asked for their help?" Jessica asked in a quiet voice, fearing she already knew the answer.

"No one would help!" he cried bitterly, bringing one hand to his face to cover his eyes. "*Maman* died a slow and painful death, and it changed my father overnight into someone I didn't know, a bitter old man. As they lowered the coffin into the ground *mon père* swore we would never again be poor, no matter what."

This part seemed to be harder for Jacques because he swallowed a few times before continuing.

"So he began to steal," he said haltingly, "first from *Maman's* rich clients, then from others, but always only from rich people—people who he thought had too much."

He took a gulp of his coffee before plunging ahead. "Papa gradually stopped being angry, and stealing became more like a game, especially when I was younger."

"Didn't it bother you that your father was a criminal?" Elizabeth asked.

Jacques shook his head.

"When I was little, I didn't know any better," he answered. "I thought it was all in fun. It was exciting to slip in and out of the big houses. And there were times when we stole so much that we could live like kings on the Riviera."

Jacques sighed and looked up at the ceiling.

"But the years took their toll. Now we live a simple life, stealing only when the money runs out." Jacques glanced at the twins, an expression of desperation on his face. "Please understand. This is the only way of life I've known since my mother passed away."

When neither Jessica nor Elizabeth spoke, Jacques shook his head hard, seemingly impatient with his own explanation.

"My father needed the emerald desperately to repay a debt," he said wearily. "I hoped only to have enough money to find him someplace warm to retire, for his health."

"And you, Jacques?" Elizabeth asked, her voice hard. "Will you keep stealing jewels and framing innocent people?"

"I deserve that," he said contritely, then sighed again. "No, I do not wish to steal anymore. Once my father is settled somewhere, I will work at something, it doesn't matter what, so long as it is an honest living."

Jacques looked down at his hands. He appeared to be trying to make a decision.

"As for now," he said quietly, "I am ready to give myself up so you and your sister can go free, Jessica."

Jessica could no longer contain herself. She flew into Jacques's arms, hugging him close, the tears spilling down her cheeks. Yes, he was a thief, and stealing was wrong. But poor Jacques, growing up without a mother! Poor Mr. Savant, whose wife died because of selfish rich people!

"I'm sorry I was so hard on you, Jacques. How terrible it must have been to lose your mother," she said. Thinking of her own loving parents back in Sweet Valley, Jessica could only begin to imagine his pain.

Jessica looked over at Elizabeth and saw tears in her sister's eyes too.

"I'm sorry," Elizabeth began, "but I have to ask. Do you have the diamond necklace?"

Jacques pushed Jessica away gently, and she reluctantly let him go.

"I must get it from my father," he said. "Will you wait here for me?" His loving look wrapped Jessica in warmth as she nodded. She heaved a deep sigh as he left the room, suddenly sure that everything would be all right.

Elizabeth's heart ached as Jacques quietly slipped from the room. She realized how lucky she was to have two parents who loved her and how difficult it would be to do without either one of them. She leaned back in her seat and wiped the tears from her eyes.

"Oh, Liz, isn't there something we can do for Jacques and his father? It's terrible that a sick old man and his young son have to go to prison," Jessica cried.

"Jacques's story is a sad one," Elizabeth admitted, "but they've been stealing for years. How would you feel if he had taken the diamond earrings Grandma gave us?"

"Not too good," Jessica said ruefully. "I'm just afraid they'll get the death penalty or something."

"Law in France is different than in America," Elizabeth said with a smile. "But I really don't think they would execute anybody for stealing. Especially if the stolen article is returned."

"How can you be so sure?" Jessica demanded. "They threw us in the dungeon without even waiting for an explanation!"

"True," Elizabeth replied slowly. "But it has to make a difference to the prince that the jewels are being returned."

Jessica's face brightened. "You may be right," she said. "And maybe you could talk to Prince Laurent, get him to help!"

Elizabeth's heart sank at the mention of Laurent. It eased her mind to know that Laurent believed in her, but that didn't change the fact that he was still engaged to Antonia.

"I'm not sure what Laurent could do," she mumbled.

Jessica instantly put an arm around Elizabeth. "I'm sorry, Liz. I didn't mean to make you feel bad by bringing up Laurent. But at least he doesn't think you're a criminal," she said brightly. "And he did spend the night trying to find you."

"I know," Elizabeth said wearily. "But Jess, he's still going to marry Antonia, no matter how he feels about me!" She felt as if she wanted to cry, but her eyes were all dried out. *It's hopeless even to think about Laurent anymore*, she told herself bitterly. *He's lost to me forever!*

Jessica squeezed her gently.

"It'll all work out, Liz, you'll see," she said

encouragingly. "And if it doesn't, just think of him spending the rest of his life with that witch, Antonia. That's a great punishment for breaking your heart."

Elizabeth had to smile then. "Yeah, I guess you're right. I wouldn't wish Antonia di Rimini on my worst enemy!"

Chapter 7

Jessica took a sip of her now cold coffee and wrinkled her nose.

"What's keeping Jacques?" she wondered out loud.

"I hope he hasn't disappeared on us," Elizabeth said ominously.

Jessica shot her an irritated glare. "Can't you cut him some slack, Liz?"

Just then Jacques burst back into the room.

"My father . . . he is gone! He left this note!"

Jessica could see Jacques's hands were trembling as he handed the note to Elizabeth. She clutched the crumpled paper in her hand, a bewildered look on her face.

"Well, Liz, what does the note say?" Jessica demanded.

She watched while Elizabeth scanned the note

quickly, then went back to the beginning for a more thorough read. Then she began to translate. "I am worried that you are getting soft, my son. I have taken the diamond necklace to satisfy our friends. If they are not repaid, they will surely seek revenge."

Jessica sat back on her chair hard. "Oh, no," she moaned aloud. "This means we have to go back to the château without the necklace. They'll put us back in the dungeon for sure!"

"Calm down," Elizabeth said sternly. "Let's think about this."

But Jessica was too distraught to think.

"Why can't we just get on the train to Paris and never look back?" She jumped up, every fiber of her being screaming to run away. "We have to get out of here!"

"Running away isn't the answer," Elizabeth said. "Besides, where would we run to?"

"Home," Jessica said immediately, her mind racing. "Jacques can go with us. If he came to Sweet Valley, he'd be safe too." *Yes*, she thought, *it's the only way. Jacques can't stay here—they'll put him in jail or maybe even kill him. The only thing left to do is get out of the country as quickly as possible.* Suddenly she noticed Elizabeth's shocked face, her mouth hanging wide open.

"What's wrong, Liz?"

"What are you talking about, Jess? We can't take Jacques back to America with this hanging over our heads!" Elizabeth jumped to her feet and waved her arms in an agitated manner. "The countess is so powerful, she could make Jacques come back, and us too for that matter. It's called *extradition*."

"No one is that powerful, Liz," Jessica sneered. "Besides, I want to go home!"

"Jessica, this isn't some movie here!" Elizabeth cried. "This is real life! And they think we're criminals!"

"All the more reason to leave!" Jessica retorted. "They're convinced, and we can't change their minds."

"We already made it look bad by escaping from the dungeon," Elizabeth went on. "It'll look even worse if we try to leave the country."

Jacques put one arm around Jessica's shoulders and squeezed gently. "Elizabeth is right, Jessica," he soothed. "America is out of the question for me."

"Don't say that!" Jessica cried, jerking away from his arm. "We're all going home! We'll be safe there!" She couldn't believe they didn't see this her way.

"No, Jessica," Jacques went on calmly and firmly. "We are going back to the château, where I will explain everything. Then all will be right again."

Suddenly Jessica understood what Jacques was saying.

"But if you explain everything, that means . . ." She turned wide eyes on him. "Do you want to be put in the dungeon?"

Jacques nodded slightly. His eyes were sad but determined. "There is no other choice," he said.

"But . . . but . . . ," Jessica stammered.

"Calm down," Elizabeth repeated, this time moving close enough to Jessica to take her hand.

"No. I refuse to let Jacques be locked away. We are going back to Sweet Valley." Jessica sat down and crossed her arms over her chest, looking straight ahead. She wasn't going to budge. There was no way she could agree to seeing the one guy she really loved give himself over to a life in prison.

Elizabeth moaned and turned her back on Jessica. Obviously Jessica's sensible sister was going to take a little more convincing. "C'mon, Liz," she exclaimed, standing up again and walking around in excitement. "Can you see Lila's face when I bring home my very own French boyfriend? She'll be positively green!"

And I can show Jacques all the hangouts, Jessica thought, her imagination taking flight. *The beach, the Dairi Burger, school. He can come watch me at cheerleading practice, maybe even take courses at the university.*

You may not know it yet, sister dear, but we are going home, and Jacques is coming with us!

Elizabeth had watched Jessica get tangled up in

her own illusions before, but this was the worst. She knew logic never worked on her sister, but it was the only weapon she had left.

"Jessica," she began, turning around to face her sister's beaming eyes. "It's going to be pretty hard to get to California with no clothes or money."

What a mess! Elizabeth thought, trying to ease her ankle into a more comfortable position. *I'm filthy, injured, and penniless, and to top it off, Jessica's finally lost it.*

Jessica didn't answer, but her determined expression didn't change either.

"Did you hear me, Jess? We have no clothes, no money!" Elizabeth insisted. "The only way out of this is to return to the château."

If we run away now, nothing will ever be the same again, Elizabeth thought. *This horrible summer will hang over the rest of our lives like a dark cloud.*

But Jessica just stared at her stupidly, almost as if Elizabeth were speaking to her in a language she didn't understand.

Elizabeth grabbed Jessica by the arms and shook her a little. "Jessica, look at me, look at yourself!" she said firmly. "We have to go back!"

Jessica's grim expression suddenly drooped, and her eyes cleared in reluctant understanding.

"OK, Liz, you can stop shaking me now," she said in a dull voice. "I guess we have to go back."

Elizabeth heaved a sigh of relief.

"Thank goodness!" she cried. She wasn't really keen on Jacques going to the dungeon, or anyone else for that matter. True, she hadn't entirely trusted him up to now, but no one deserved to be in that cold, dank, musty place. It was like something out of the Middle Ages! And Jacques seemed somehow different, more sincere. There was no more of that phony French moonlight in his voice.

But now Jessica was staring at her unhappily. "I can't believe how insensitive you are, Liz," she said, a sob catching her voice. "Jacques is going to the dungeon, but you don't care one bit. If it were Prince Laurent being sent up the river, you'd be bawling your eyes out right now!"

"We don't know that Jacques is going to the dungeon," Elizabeth insisted. "We won't know anything until we go back to the château."

"That's right," Jacques said. "But there is one thing I *will* promise you, Jessica. Even if I do go to prison, it is not the end for us."

Elizabeth was warmed by Jacques's compassion for her sister's feelings, and she smiled slightly. She was grateful that she wasn't the only logical person in the room. *Maybe I really did misjudge him after all,* she thought. *But I'm still not letting him out of my sight until our names are cleared!*

"Come on," Elizabeth said, hoisting herself to her feet with her makeshift crutch. "We might as well get this over with."

"All right," Jessica said grudgingly. She reached

out a hand and helped Elizabeth get her balance.

Jacques shook his head and smiled sadly. "You must not leave my country in disgrace, Jessica," he pointed out.

Jessica suddenly threw her arms around Jacques's neck.

"I can't believe you're actually going to confess!" she cried. "I don't understand why there isn't some way to prove that we're innocent without having to turn you in!"

Jacques removed himself from Jessica's grasp and smiled at her sadly again. Then he walked over and opened the door, holding it as the twins passed through.

"Everything will be fine, Jess," Elizabeth said as she hobbled into the hallway. Relief coursed through her tired body. She was just glad that they were on their way.

I'm going to get a chance to explain everything to Laurent. No matter what else happens, he'll always know I was innocent.

Prince Laurent lifted his chin slightly so his valet, François, could button the top button of the formal uniform he was wearing to the upcoming press conference. True to his word, he had allowed his father to invite reporters from all over the country so they could be there when he announced his official engagement to Antonia di Rimini.

"If I may say so, sir," François began deferentially,

"you look very fine this morning. This must be a happy day for you." François was a short, stout man in his early forties, with graying hair at his temples and an absolute sense of what to say and do at the perfect time. Laurent had known him all his life.

"Thank you," Laurent replied automatically. "Of course it is." Laurent frowned, sad that he could not confide his real feelings even to his own valet, a man who had known him since birth.

Every piece of clothing he wore was heavily braided in gold, with epaulets and shiny buttons and military medals that he hadn't earned but that his rank allowed him. Never before had the formal court dress weighed him down so. But he knew it was really his spirit that was so heavy.

His future stretched out before him—marrying Antonia, having children, ruling the country—a great dark span of years filled with duty and responsibility. And all without the one thing he most desired, the love of Elizabeth Wakefield.

"Did Miss Antonia like the ring you gave her this morning?" François asked. He was busy brushing and examining Laurent's tuxedo, which he would need for the betrothal celebration that night. Laurent knew that François would make sure his evening clothes were perfect.

"She was . . . appropriately pleased," Laurent said carefully. Actually, when he gave her the ring shortly after breakfast, she had let out an ear-piercing screech. In a split second she had flown out of her chair and practically strangled him with a hug, smearing her garish lipstick all over his cheeks with her kisses.

He could not imagine how she would be able to function as the wife of an international political leader. *At our first state dinner she will probably jump up and down when she shakes hands with some dignitary,* he thought ruefully.

Still, it was better to follow his father's directions in order to free Elizabeth and her sister from the countess's evil designs. At least he would always know that Elizabeth was free to pursue her own dreams.

Laurent waved François away from giving his uniform one last brushing and left his rooms to meet his parents on the large terrace outside. Everything had been set up for the press conference. When he emerged from the château, cameras flashed wildly and microphones were thrust in his face as reporters fired questions at him.

He ignored them all and made his way toward his parents. They were standing to the side of a podium with the Countess di Rimini. His father wore military dress identical to his own, complete with braid and medals. The countess wore a tailored yellow linen suit that barely disguised her bulges. His stepmother was smartly turned out in a flattering two-piece suit in a lovely shade of green. The countess posed herself with an eye to the many cameras that flashed here and there.

"Father, Stepmother, Countess," Laurent greeted them, nodding slightly.

"You look very handsome, Laurent," his stepmother commented.

"Yes, son," his father said approvingly. "We are all awaiting your important announcement."

"I will remain true to my word, Father," he said in a careful tone. It would never do for his heart's pain to come through in his public speaking voice. The countess said nothing, as if daring him to back out.

Antonia waited for Laurent at the podium, dressed in a rather outrageous red suit, cut low across the bosom. She held her head high, nose in the air, plainly triumphant. Occasionally she moved her left hand so the sun could glint off her new ring. *That's hardly an appropriate outfit in which to announce an engagement,* Laurent thought. *Elizabeth would never wear something like that!*

Laurent approached the podium and leaned down slightly toward the microphone.

"May I have your attention, please?" His voice boomed out over the expectant crowd. A chorus of whispers and "Shhhs" greeted his request. He looked back at his parents before beginning, and their pride shone on their faces. He wished he could feel the same about what he was now going to do.

When all was quiet, he began in French. "It is my honor and pleasure to announce today my

109

betrothal to Antonia di Rimini." There were more flashing lights and buzzing comments, and all Laurent could think of was Elizabeth's sweet face, her sea blue eyes, the way she moved in unconscious, graceful gestures.

If anyone looks or acts like a princess, it's Elizabeth, he thought. He couldn't help comparing his lovely, elegant Elizabeth with the shrill, coarse, self-centered Antonia. Then he mentally shook himself in order to be able to answer the reporters' questions, pointing to one persistent woman who had her hand raised.

The reporter opened her mouth to speak but was cut off.

"Look!" someone shouted suddenly, and all heads turned. Stumbling across the lawn, in their dirty, torn ball gowns, blond hair in matted tangles, came Elizabeth and Jessica.

Laurent almost called out to Elizabeth in joy but snapped his mouth shut when he saw someone emerge from the woods behind the twins.

It was Jacques Landeau.

Chapter 8

Elizabeth leaned on Jessica and Jacques as they made their way toward the château. Her heart leapt into her throat when she saw the vast array of reporters and cameramen arranged on the front lawn.

"Oh, no, they must be announcing the theft and identifying us as fugitives!" she exclaimed in panic.

She lost her grip on the crutch, and it clunked to the ground. Jacques quickly scooped it up before she could lose her balance and placed it in her hand.

"Do you think so?" Jessica asked, glancing down at her worn, filthy dress. "I don't want any reporters taking pictures of me in this ratty old ball gown!"

They stopped abruptly when the whole crowd turned in their direction. Elizabeth felt as if the eyes of the entire world were on her, and in a corner of her mind she realized this must be how Laurent felt every day. It was how he lived his life—under a microscope.

Then Elizabeth noticed the Countess di Rimini and Antonia openly smiling, almost puffed out with happiness. *Oh, no,* Elizabeth thought, tears welling in her tired eyes. She scanned Antonia's left hand, and sure enough, a huge diamond engagement ring glittered there in the sunlight.

Antonia looked down her nose at Elizabeth and smiled smugly. She raised her left hand and wiggled the ring finger until Elizabeth was almost blinded by the reflection of the sun off the twinkling diamond.

"What a tasteless witch she is!" Jessica said into Elizabeth's ear. "I bet even Lila would think that ring was too much!"

Elizabeth didn't care what Lila thought. "How could he?" she moaned under her breath. Numbly she looked at Laurent.

Laurent lowered his eyes quickly to stare at his clenched hands, as if he were ashamed to face her, but Elizabeth had already seen the evidence of his broken heart written across his features.

"It makes me sick," she said to Jessica, her pain mingling with outrage that she had so misjudged Laurent. "He's trading his happiness for his duty. Why doesn't he stand up for himself? He's nothing but a coward."

But even as she said the words, Elizabeth knew

they weren't true. It was just the hurt talking. Laurent was a brave and wonderful person. And she knew he loved her. There must be some other reason he had agreed to marry Antonia and leave Elizabeth behind.

But why, Laurent? Elizabeth asked him silently. *What could make you throw away our love?*

Elizabeth slumped a little after her outburst, and Jessica wrapped her arm more tightly around her sister's shoulders. She glanced over Elizabeth's head at Jacques, and he locked eyes with her.

"Take care of Elizabeth, Jessica," Jacques said firmly. "I'll do the rest." Then he started across the lawn.

Elizabeth leaned against her heavily, and without Jacques's support Jessica nearly fell over. It seemed as if Jacques was moving in slow motion, taking one step after another, moving toward the podium, every head turning to follow him.

"Jess, you're hurting me," she heard Elizabeth say. She looked down at where she gripped Elizabeth's arm and saw how tightly her fingers were wrapped around it. She loosened up a little and looked back toward the podium.

Jacques had finally reached the terrace. Jessica wanted to scream as Jacques politely asked Laurent to step away from the podium. *He can't do this, he can't do this!* she thought frantically. *How can I stop him? Should I just run up and shove him aside?*

But Jacques was already speaking in French. "What is he saying?" she asked Elizabeth.

"He's apologizing for the interruption," Elizabeth explained in a low voice. "And he's saying that we never stole anything."

"Yes, yes, I just heard our names!" she said impatiently. "What else?"

"He's admitting he stole the emerald and the diamond necklace. I can't believe it!" Elizabeth continued. "Somehow I didn't think he would go through with his confession."

"I have to go up there," Jessica said. She looked around frantically for something for Elizabeth to sit on. She grabbed one of the chairs from the cluster where the reporters had been sitting and dumped Elizabeth into it.

"Wait here!" she hissed and then sprinted forward as the guards came to claim their prisoner. "Don't hurt him!" she cried desperately in English.

The guards didn't seem to hear her. They grabbed Jacques by each arm and almost pulled him off his feet as they dragged him away from the podium. Jessica looked at the royal family, but the prince and princess were only shaking their heads sadly.

Laurent seemed to be in a state of shock. The countess's expression alternated between triumph and consternation. It seemed to Jessica that she

114

couldn't make up her mind whether to be happy that the real thief had confessed or upset that it hadn't been Jessica and her sister after all.

Jessica knew she would get no help from anyone on that terrace. She followed the guards as best she could, dodging in and out among the reporters and photographers who were stampeding in an attempt to get a statement from Jacques. *Evidently,* Jessica thought, *his confession is even more newsworthy than Prince Laurent's announcement.*

But the guards wouldn't let anyone get near Jacques. They managed to drag him into the château. Jessica knew they would throw him into the dungeon, probably into the same cell Jessica had shared with Elizabeth. Somehow she had to get in there and see him . . . if only to say good-bye!

Jacques knew he would be taken away once he made his announcement, but he had no idea the guards would be so swift or so rough. He just managed to catch Jessica's eye and mouth the words "I love you" before they hauled him to a back entrance of the château. The last thing he saw before they closed the door was a sea of unfamiliar faces . . . the reporters from the press conference who were screaming questions and taking pictures.

The guards dragged him down a long flight of

jagged steps into a dark cellar, where they pushed him into a cold, stone cell and slammed the door shut.

"Dirty thief!" the taller guard spat at him in French before they both disappeared.

Now what? Jacques pulled himself off the floor and sat on the cot. It was lumpy and uncomfortable but better than the floor. The one window in the tiny cell was high on the wall, but by standing on the cot on tiptoes he could just see outside.

It seemed incredible that the sun could still be shining and that a tangy sea breeze could find its way into this dank cell. He wondered what Jessica was doing. Was she worried about him? Would she try to see him?

Everything Jacques had was gone, except for Jessica. At least he hoped he still had Jessica. His father would never come near the château. It was too great a risk. Jacques had no other family or friends. Just Jessica. He hoped she would at least try to visit him.

At least his father was safe. The dungeon was a cold, smelly, damp place, and Jacques figured prison would be no better. His father's health would never withstand being locked up in a cell like this. It was better that Jacques should be locked away. Perhaps there wouldn't be a long sentence. He could still be a relatively young man when he got out.

But who was he kidding? With the countess

involved, he had no reason to hope for leniency. No, he might as well face it. His life was over.

Although he hadn't cried since his mother died years ago, Jacques sat back down on the cot and buried his face in his hands, tears falling between his fingers.

As Laurent watched Jacques being dragged away he felt as if he were dreaming. *None of this is happening,* Laurent thought. *It can't be.*

Now that this Jacques person had come forward, the reason for Laurent's engagement had vanished. The girls were no longer under suspicion of theft, so he had agreed to this idiotic engagement for no reason.

But now the damage was done. The whole world had heard about the betrothal. It would be humiliating for his family and Antonia's if he backed out now. For the sake of propriety he would have to throw his life away.

Elizabeth was still sitting on the chair that Jessica had found for her, and Laurent noticed for the first time that one of her ankles was bound with a bandage. Elizabeth was hurt! More than ever he wished he could gather her in his arms and swear to her his undying devotion.

Her eyes were so sad. Anxious to erase the pain he saw there, Laurent began to move off the terrace in her direction. Elizabeth, however, shook her head ever so slightly. She stood shakily and spoke to a nearby guard, who then began to help her into the château. Now that she was no longer a suspect, the guard seemed only too happy to help. As Laurent watched her limp away, his heart constricted. *This is the worst day of my life,* he thought in despair.

Suddenly a hand grabbed his arm. He looked down into Antonia's upturned, beaming face.

"At long last," she said in a loud, shrill voice, "we're officially engaged!"

Laurent could only nod.

"And we'll have the most beautiful wedding," she went on, apparently unaware of his total revulsion. "The attendants will all be in blue. What do you think of a spring wedding?"

"Fine," he said in a bland voice, wishing he could jerk his arm from her grasp. Her touch made his skin crawl.

"Son," the countess said, embracing him stiffly. "Welcome to our family."

His stepmother embraced him formally, and then his father stepped up. As he too embraced Laurent he said into his ear, "And your Elizabeth is cleared completely, it seems."

"Yes, Father," Laurent said in a tired voice. "So it would seem."

"And our children will be absolutely gorgeous. . . ." Antonia was still gushing at his side, making him cringe.

Laurent patted her hand absently, thinking, *I*

have to listen to that voice for the rest of my life. I don't know if I can stand it. Maybe I'll travel, make a lot of state visits and leave her at home with the children. Maybe I'll encourage her to visit her mother frequently . . . without me. Maybe I'll lose my hearing early and never, ever get a hearing aid!

Chapter 9

Jessica raced up the stairs ahead of Elizabeth, anxious to take a shower and change her clothes. She desperately wanted to visit Jacques in the dungeon, but not before she got rid of that tattered, dirty ball gown. And her hair! It was a veritable rat's nest.

As the hot water beat down on her back Jessica put her mind to work on the problem of getting Jacques out of the dungeon. The fact that he freely confessed to the theft of the emerald and the diamond bracelet just had to mean something to the countess and the prince and princess. And what about Jacques's father? He was to blame too.

As Jessica was drying her hair the guard helped Elizabeth into the room.

"That's a good idea," Elizabeth said once the guard was gone. "I could use a shower too."

"Can you manage with your ankle?" Jessica

asked, hoping Elizabeth wouldn't need her help. She didn't want Jacques to languish in the dungeon any longer than necessary before knowing she still cared about him.

Elizabeth smiled wearily. "Planning on a visit to Jacques?"

"How can you tell? Is it that obvious?" Jessica asked almost sheepishly.

"Yep." Elizabeth nodded, lowering herself onto the bed and smiling slightly at the gaurd as he turned to leave. "But I can take my shower without you. I feel so crummy, I won't even notice the pain if I can just get clean."

"Did you talk to Laurent?" Jessica had to ask, even if it hurt Elizabeth to talk about it. It wouldn't be good for her to brood about her feelings alone.

"No," Elizabeth said, and Jessica could tell she was trying hard not to cry. "Antonia was looking pretty possessive, so I decided to just come up here."

"Maybe he won't marry her after all," Jessica offered, but the words sounded lame. "I'm sorry about all this, Liz."

Elizabeth managed a crooked smile. "I'll be all right. But you better get going if you want to see Jacques."

Jessica smiled as she put the last finishing touches on her hair. She tossed it from side to side, admiring the way it billowed in golden waves. Perfect!

"Well, Liz, wish me luck."

"You're not going to try to break him out, are you?" Elizabeth asked in a shocked voice.

"No, I need luck just getting *in*," Jessica explained. "If the guard is the same one we had, it'll be hopeless."

"OK, OK, good luck!" Elizabeth shook her head as Jessica bounced from the room.

Jessica took the back stairs down to the dungeon entrance, not wanting to explain to anyone where she was going. She stared down to where the guard stood at the bottom of the stairs. Jessica let out a sigh of relief when she saw that a different guard was on duty.

This one was younger and more handsome than the first. He had reddish brown hair and an attractive mustache, and his broad shoulders tapered down to a trim waist. He watched her come down the steps, his gray eyes alert but not unfriendly. In fact, when she got to the bottom of the stairs, he actually smiled at her.

"May I please speak to the prisoner?" Jessica asked in her carefully rehearsed French.

"I am not sure that is a good idea," the guard said, but his expression was still friendly and open.

"Oh, please," she said in her most honey sweet voice. "Only for a moment. *Un moment, s'il vous plaît?*" She hoped he thought her French accent was cute enough to grant her request.

"You have no files or skeleton keys, no?" he asked in halting English.

Jessica beamed her best innocent smile at him. "No, sir."

"Then you may see him," the guard said, pointing toward the cell.

She walked down the hallway, shuddering at the memory of having been locked up in the place. The walls dripped damp slime, and the cold came right through the soles of her shoes. When she got to the cell and peered inside, she saw Jacques stretched out on the cot, staring up at the ceiling. He looked so lost and forlorn that her heart ached.

"Jacques?" she asked tentatively.

Jacques jumped from the cot, and his whole face lit up when he saw her.

"I was hoping you would be able to come down to see me," he said. "Did you have trouble getting in here?"

"No," she answered, leaning her hands against the wooden door so she could get closer to the small, barred window. "But Jacques, it broke my heart when they dragged you away! Did they hurt you? Are you all right? Did they say anything about a trial?"

Jacques smiled sadly at her and reached a single finger between .the bars to stroke her chin gently.

"There will be no trial, my dear Jessica," he said. "I confessed, so there is no need for a trial.

They will merely sentence me, probably to life in prison."

"Oh, no!" she cried, stricken at the thought of such a harsh sentence. "They can't do that! Surely it counts that you confessed on your own. How can they be so unfair?"

She could feel the tears start at the thought of this young man spending the rest of his days behind bars. That could be sixty years or more!

Jacques sighed. "It is up to the judge, *ma chérie.*"

Jessica was suddenly angry. "It's not like you killed someone! You stole some crummy jewelry, and you can just give it back. Doesn't that make a difference?"

"You make it sound so simple, my sweet Jessica," he said ruefully.

Jessica's mind raced as she tried to think of a way to help Jacques. How could she make the prince go easier on him?

"Maybe my sister could talk to Prince Laurent," she offered. "He could beg his father to have mercy on you."

Jacques shook his head. "Jessica, you do not understand. Stealing from the countess, who represents a foreign government, is an international crime," he tried to explain patiently. "The countess would be dishonored before the whole world if she did not pursue a heavy sentence."

Jessica tossed her head defiantly. "The countess! That old cow should be put away herself!"

Jacques reached his fingers through the bars, and Jessica grasped them in her own.

"She might retaliate against this government," he continued. "And no one will take that risk."

"Wait!" Jessica said as another possibility popped into her head. "What about *your* father? If your father gave back the diamond and the emerald and tried to make some kind of deal . . ."

"I will never go to my father!" Jacques cried. Jessica jerked her hand away from his in shock. "I will protect my father to the end of my life," he added more quietly.

"I'm sorry, Jacques," Jessica began, but he cut her off.

"And you must promise never to ask me again to betray my father," he said firmly. "He is the only family I have left. You must swear to keep the truth about my father a secret."

"I swear," Jessica said in a small voice, completely subdued by the force of Jacques's plea.

"You must swear on your sister's life, Jessica," he insisted.

He's so sexy when he's intense like this, Jessica thought, her heart thumping.

"All right, Jacques," she said quietly. "I love you enough to do what you ask. I swear to you on my sister's life that I will not say anything about your father."

Laurent thought the betrothal dinner would

never end. With Antonia clutching his right hand and the countess crowding him on the left, he could hardly even eat.

The executive chef had positively outdone himself, with the first course of baby artichoke hearts in a delicate lemon sauce, a course of grilled fresh salmon, and a main course of tender beef in a flaky pastry crust. The wine flowed freely, and everyone but Laurent was tipsy by the time the meal was halfway over.

Of course, food was the last thing on his mind. All he could think about was the way Elizabeth had turned away from him that afternoon. Even the messages he'd sent up to her room had gone unanswered.

"Oh, Laurent, you have made me the happiest girl in the world," Antonia gushed into his right ear.

"You made the right choice, young man," the countess thundered from his left.

The right choice. The words echoed in Laurent's mind, mocking him. *I haven't made the right choice. I haven't made any choice at all*, he thought. All he wanted was Elizabeth. Instead he had Antonia . . . and his honor. What good was honor when he was destined to be miserable the rest of his life?

Laurent chewed slowly and let his mind wander. *It's true, I don't have to marry Antonia now that Elizabeth is out of danger. What's the worst that can happen if I refuse? My country will suffer scandal. Antonia and her mother will be humiliated. My parents . . .* His heart lurched in his chest at the thought of the reaction his father and stepmother would have if he refused to go through with the wedding.

"Laurent," Antonia whined in his ear, "you're not paying any attention to me at all!"

"I'm sorry, Antonia," he said woodenly. "It's been a long and exhausting day."

"But your father said there would be dancing after dinner," she said petulantly.

Laurent looked into Antonia's eyes, and it hit him like a thunderbolt. *I will not marry this girl,* he thought suddenly. *I don't have to, and I will not.* All that remained was for him to tell his father and stepmother, and that would take all his courage.

All his life Laurent had been a dutiful son. Now he would be defying centuries of tradition for the sake of the most beautiful girl he had ever known. A shiver ran down his spine and his stomach flopped over at the thought. All he had to do was tell his parents, then he would be free to love the only girl who'd ever managed to capture his heart!

Though the coming confrontation filled him with dread, the night no longer seemed so unbearable to Laurent. He was even able to dance with Antonia without too much revulsion, knowing he wouldn't have to spend the rest of his life with her.

When the dancing was finally over, Laurent returned to his rooms to find François waiting patiently.

"I must talk with my parents tonight," he said without preamble. "You may retire if you wish."

"Is anything wrong, sir?" the other man asked, concern in his voice and etched on his face.

Laurent was touched by the valet's reaction. "It is very kind of you to ask, François, but I am fine. There is so much going on, I am feeling distracted," he half lied.

"Very good, sir. If you need anything, please call," François said, bowing slightly and gliding out of the room.

Later, as Laurent went to his parents' private quarters to tell them his decision, he nearly lost his nerve. *What am I doing? How can I go against their wishes? This is my country's future I'm deciding, not just my own!* At the door he almost turned away without knocking. Then Elizabeth's face came to mind, and he lifted his fist and knocked firmly.

His father was relaxing in a chair before a blazing fire in the fireplace, smoking his pipe. He was wearing his favorite emerald-colored smoking jacket with gold trim, and his reading glasses were perched on the end of his nose. He held a sheaf of papers in his hand.

His stepmother was seated directly opposite, in the other chair beside the fireplace. The princess was dressed in a graceful caftan of royal blue silk. She too wore glasses in order to see the tiny decorative stitches she was placing in her linen sampler. He knew her motto was, A true lady never sits idle.

"Father, Stepmother," he said. He took a deep breath, hoping they would someday forgive him. "I will not marry Antonia."

"What?" his father asked sharply. He stood up from his chair and set the papers he had been reading aside. He pulled off his glasses and looked at Laurent, one eye squinting slightly. "What are you saying, Laurent?"

"I will not marry Antonia. . . . I—I cannot marry her. . . . I don't love her. . . ." He hated the way he stammered in the face of his father's anger.

Princess Catherine was frowning. She had remained motionless after Laurent's announcement, but now she calmly set aside her needlework.

"Laurent, I thought you had decided once and for all. How can you humiliate us this way?" she asked sternly.

"Father, we made an agreement," Laurent pushed himself to say. "But now that we know Elizabeth and her sister are innocent of wrongdoing, there is no need for the agreement or the engagement." The simple mention of Elizabeth's name seemed to give him greater strength. "And I find I cannot tolerate the thought of being married to Antonia!"

"Do not raise your voice to me!" his father

thundered. "You are defying me for the sake of that American girl? Do you think we would permit you to marry her?"

"It's not just because of Elizabeth, Father," Laurent tried desperately to explain. "It also has to do with what I want, how I feel about marriage. If I am to live with someone for the rest of my life, I must love her!"

"Love! *Bah!*" The prince slashed the air with his arm. "Love is a fleeting, illusory thing that soon passes. It is the day-to-day companionship, reliance on each other. . . ." He wiped his face with one hand. "You are too young to understand!"

"I am *not* too young to know my own mind," Laurent asserted. "Whether or not I marry Elizabeth is not the point. The point is I don't want to marry Antonia!"

"Oh, how humiliated Antonia and the countess will be!" his stepmother moaned. "I can only imagine how they will retaliate. Did you think of that?"

"It is no use," Laurent said, valiantly pushing forward. "If they do not suffer this little humiliation now, Antonia and I will both be miserable for the rest of our lives. I don't love Antonia, and I don't think I ever could. I don't even *like* her. I'm sure she wouldn't want that kind of relationship any more than I would." Laurent wasn't really sure about that, but it sounded good.

"Love! Love!" his father stormed. "You are obsessed with this romantic notion of marrying for love!"

"It's not just a romantic notion, Father," Laurent insisted. "Millions of people all over the world will marry only for love. I merely want to be one of them!"

"Millions of people . . . ," his father sputtered. "Commoners, all of them! We are the royal family, we make alliances! You cannot afford to give your own wishes any credence!" He paced up and down a few steps. "Why would you want to act like a commoner?"

Laurent knew he wouldn't win in a shouting match with his father, but then a thought came to him that gave him courage. "But Father," Laurent asked in his quietest voice, "didn't you marry for love the second time around?"

His father suddenly stopped and looked at Laurent, a surprised look on his face. There was a thick silence in the room for a moment or two. When the prince spoke again, it was much more quietly under the watchful eyes of the princess.

"Yes, my son," he said reluctantly, "I did."

"And you are happy with my stepmother?" Laurent continued, immediately sensing he had hit on the perfect argument.

"Yes, yes." The prince's shoulders slumped a little, and he sighed. "I am beginning to see your point. Perhaps, Laurent, we have been unfair to you, trying to impose outdated traditions."

Laurent felt his heart soar at his father's words. "Thank you, Father," he acknowledged with a smile.

The older man approached Laurent and put an arm around his shoulders. "I will do what I can to reason with the countess," his father said wearily. "I am sure you know what her reaction will be."

Suddenly the countess burst through the closed door.

"He will not have to wait to see my reaction!" she thundered. "How can you break my daughter's heart like this!"

The prince and princess were momentarily shocked, their mouths hanging open.

"Were you listening at the door?" the prince demanded.

"That's not important!" the countess shrieked. "Don't bother me with ridiculous details!"

Laurent moved forward to intercept the countess. "Please," he began, "it was never my intention—"

"You are a disrespectful young man who needs to be taught a lesson!" she boomed at him.

"Why don't we all calm down?" Princess Catherine pleaded softly. "Let us all be rational and discuss this like adults."

"Discuss!" the countess huffed. "I demand that you force this shameless young man to marry Antonia!"

The prince's face hardened at the countess's words.

"He is neither disrespectful nor shameless, Countess," he said in a tone that said he expected not to be challenged. "Perhaps it is time to accept the modern way of doing some things. We no longer live in the Middle Ages. Perhaps with Laurent we should begin redefining our traditions."

Laurent shot his father a grateful glance. It was the last thing he would have expected, to hear his father defending a point of view so new to him. And yet here he was, acting as if it had been his idea all along!

"Well, I *never!*" the countess cried. "This matter is by no means decided," she shouted over her shoulder as she flounced from the room.

And Laurent was afraid she meant it.

Chapter 10

The next morning Elizabeth sat by the window in her chamber, the sunlight streaming down over her. It was good to feel clean again, and her soft cotton shorts and simple, short-sleeved shirt were infinitely better than the ball gown. Even the memory of that filthy, torn rag was enough to make her shudder.

The warmth of the sun felt good, especially on her sore ankle. The court doctor said it wasn't a bad sprain but that she should rest it as much as possible. That meant Jessica had to do most of the work with the children.

Normally Elizabeth would have been secretly pleased that her sister was being forced to take on some responsibility. It seemed as if every time they started a project together, Elizabeth ended up doing all the work.

But this summer had been different. Elizabeth had shirked her duties more than once in order to spend time with Laurent. On a couple of occasions, when it was her turn to take the kids, Elizabeth hadn't shown up at all. And now she felt incredibly guilty that Jessica had all the responsibility yet again. *Of course,* she thought with a wistful smile, *it's really all Laurent's fault. If he hadn't been so handsome and charming . . .*

"Why did I have to go and think of Laurent?" Elizabeth groaned. Her eyes quickly filled with tears. *I wonder what he's doing this morning. How can he even think about marrying Antonia when he loves me? What good is a tradition that forces you to ruin your life?*

Elizabeth jumped as a soft knock on the door broke into her reverie. She didn't really want to see anyone, but then she heard Pierre's tiny voice. "Mademoiselle Elizabeth, please let me to come in."

"All right, Pierre," she said resignedly, wiping her eyes with the backs of her hands.

Pierre looked very solemn when he entered the room. He walked right over to Elizabeth, threw his little arms around her neck, and hugged her hard.

"I am sorry you are so sad," he whispered in her ear.

Elizabeth was touched by his concern. "That's

very sweet, Pierre," she said, struggling not to cry again. "Thank you." Gazing at Pierre's thick, wavy dark hair and soft brown eyes, Elizabeth could have been looking at Laurent as a child. She felt a sudden sharp pang in her heart. Would she ever see her prince again?

Pierre plopped onto Elizabeth's bed and crossed his legs under him.

"Can I do something to cheer you?" he asked, his small upturned face hopeful.

Elizabeth managed a slight smile. "Sometimes it takes a while for a person to feel better after they are hurt," she tried to explain. "But I'll be fine."

"Are you going to marry my brother?" Pierre asked hopefully.

Elizabeth's heart lurched. His expression was so innocent, she could hardly bear to tell him the truth.

"Laurent is going to marry Antonia," she said delicately.

"But I hate Antonia!" Pierre said vehemently. "I do not want her for my sister!"

Elizabeth wiped fresh tears from the corners of her eyes. "Things don't always work out the way we want, Pierre," she told him sadly.

"I want you!" he said boldly. "You would be a good princess."

"Thank you, Pierre. That's very nice of you," she said simply. She turned to gaze out the window again so he wouldn't see the pain written on her face.

"*Pardonnez-moi.*"

Elizabeth jumped slightly when she heard a voice that made her skin crawl. She looked up to find the countess standing in the open doorway.

"I must speak with you, my dear," the older woman said, entering the room without being asked. Her voice was honey sweet, a tone Elizabeth hadn't thought her capable of using.

The countess was dressed in a stylish black suit with a filmy, bright green silk blouse that actually complemented her hair. For the first time since Elizabeth had seen her on the train weeks ago, the countess seemed subdued and calm. It made Elizabeth suspicious.

"Pierre," Elizabeth said, reaching over to ruffle his hair. "Why don't you so downstairs and play with your sisters? I'll see you later."

"OK," he answered, jumping off the bed. He scrambled quickly out of the room, and Elizabeth knew he was glad for the opportunity to get away from the countess. She wished she were so lucky.

"May I help you?" Elizabeth inquired in her iciest tone of voice. She wished she could stand and look the countess in the eyes. Sitting on her bed, she felt powerless against the awful woman's imposing form.

"I came to apologize for accusing you and

137

your sister of theft," the countess began.

"Thank you," Elizabeth said shortly, refusing to let down her guard. She didn't believe the apology for a minute. *What can she really want from me?* Elizabeth thought, eyeing the countess warily.

"You must be very happy," the countess went on. "First the charges were dropped against you, and now Laurent has called off his engagement to my daughter."

"H-He . . . he what?" Elizabeth gasped, and her hand flew up to cover her mouth. She nearly jumped up and shouted with joy. Laurent wasn't getting married after all! Suddenly she was overflowing with excitement. Her hands were shaking, and her heart was hammering against her chest. Could it really be true? Had Laurent actually stood up to his parents?

Elizabeth struggled to keep her emotions in check, not wanting the countess to see her so flustered.

The countess looked her up and down, a slight sneer on her face.

"In fact," the countess continued, "after you were absolved, he hardly waited a moment before breaking my daughter's heart."

"What do you mean, 'after I was absolved'?" Elizabeth asked slowly. What did her innocence have to do with Laurent's decision to break with tradition?

"You see," the countess said, peering down her nose at Elizabeth, "he only agreed to marry my Antonia when I promised to drop the charges against you and your sister. Now that you have been proven innocent, he has backed out on his agreement. Laurent seems unable to stay true to his word."

Elizabeth's heart flipped. Laurent had been ready to throw his life away in order to save Elizabeth and her sister. She couldn't believe the sacrifice he had almost made for her! How could she have misjudged him, thinking he had allowed himself to be bullied by tradition? He had only been trying to help her all along. And now he had finally defied his father and taken charge of his life. Elizabeth felt her face flush with pride.

But the countess wouldn't let her stay happy for long. She began to walk around the room, her high heels clicking on the wooden floor.

"You know," she began again, still speaking in a reasonable voice, "this kind of international affront can lead to bad blood between governments. It would be terrible, wouldn't it, to be the cause of an international incident?" she asked pointedly, turning and staring directly into Elizabeth's eyes.

Elizabeth felt her brave front begin to crack as the full implication of the countess's words sank in.

"What kind of incident?" she asked, fighting to keep the fear out of her voice.

"Trade wars, embargoes. There could be all kinds of political implications," the countess answered matter-of-factly.

Elizabeth felt a rising panic take control of her emotions. The severity of the countess's thinly cloaked threat overwhelmed Elizabeth as her thoughts rushed along at lightning speed.

Could something as trivial as one broken engagement really have that kind of effect on the relationship between two countries that had been allies for years? As Elizabeth looked into the countess's smug face she realized that the horrid woman actually meant to act on her threats. *If I had never come to the château, Laurent would have married Antonia and none of this would have happened.* Elizabeth had no doubt that Laurent's love for her had given him the strength to stand up to his father.

If I were to leave, she thought slowly, *maybe Laurent would go through with his agreement with the countess. Maybe he would see that it's the only way to secure the future of his country. But if he* does *marry Antonia, he will never be happy.* For the first time Elizabeth truly understood the pressure that Laurent had been forced to endure his whole life.

"Naturally," the countess said smoothly, "if Laurent wasn't 'distracted,' he would be happy to marry Antonia and avoid any ugly incidents."

Elizabeth knew that this was the point the countess had been trying to make all along.

"Countess," she said quickly, summoning up her strength. "Your little mission has been accomplished. Now if you'll excuse me, I have some things to attend to." She stood up, hobbled over to the door, and opened it, facing the countess with her chin held high.

The countess flashed a triumphant smile.

"Of course, my dear," she said in that awful, fake voice. She floated out of the room, looking smugly satisfied.

As soon as the countess was gone Elizabeth sprang into action. She had to get out of the château . . . *now*. The only way to prevent the "international incident" that the countess had alluded to was for Elizabeth to disappear. *Laurent will do what's right*, she thought, frantically pulling clothing from her dresser drawers. *As soon as I'm out of the picture, he'll know what he has to do.*

Elizabeth hobbled around her tower room, packing her bags without bothering to fold things neatly the way she usually did. She tossed her T-shirts, shorts, and jeans into her suitcase in one jumbled pile, then dumped her brush, journal, and few cosmetics on top, mashing the whole mess down with the palm of her hand.

Elizabeth somehow got the clasp fastened,

pushed her hair impatiently away from her eyes, and used her new crutch to hop out the door. The suitcase was heavy, and Elizabeth stumbled a few times as she negotiated her way down the narrow staircase. Near the bottom her crutch fell to the floor with a clatter, and Elizabeth had to hop the rest of the way.

A startled young servant stood at the base of the stairs, holding the fallen crutch. Elizabeth reached out and snatched it from the girl, alarming her unintentionally.

"*S'il vous plaît,*" Elizabeth said, trying to keep her voice calm. She hoped her French wouldn't desert her in her agitated state. "I need a car to take me to the train station."

Luckily the servant composed herself quickly. "Of course, mademoiselle," she offered with a smile. "It will only be a moment."

Elizabeth carried her suitcase through the corridors, grateful that she didn't bump into anyone she knew. *I hope Jessica will understand,* Elizabeth thought fervently. She wished there was time to go to the nursery and explain. But she had to get out of there as quickly as possible, before Laurent came to see her and realized she was gone. She left the château by the servants' entrance and waited for the car to come.

Gaston, the same chauffeur who'd picked Elizabeth and Jessica up at the train station when they first arrived, pulled the car around the corner.

He smiled brightly at Elizabeth as he stepped out of the car.

"Leaving us, mademoiselle?" he asked in his excellent English. He popped the trunk and placed her bag inside, then opened the door to the backseat.

"Yes, Gaston. There is . . . an emergency at home," she lied, slipping into the car. "Jessica will be staying to complete our job, but I must go home."

Gaston leaned over and looked at her through the open window as he closed the door behind her. His brow puckered into a frown.

"Does this have to do with that accusation . . . that you and your sister stole some jewels?" he asked carefully.

Elizabeth felt herself blush up to the roots of her hair. "That was all a misunderstanding," she said, wishing he would just get into the car and drive. "They caught the real thief. Didn't you hear?"

"Of course," Gaston replied. "But I would hate for you to leave France because of such a misunderstanding. You might never wish to come back."

He has no idea how right he is, she thought.

"I'll be back someday," she said, willing to say anything to get them on their way. "But right now I really need to get to the train station."

"Good. I am glad. I hope you enjoyed your stay with us, mademoiselle," Gaston said with a smile.

He finally walked around to the driver's side and got in.

"Yes, yes," Elizabeth said impatiently. She hoped he wouldn't want to chat all the way to the train station. Gaston must have sensed her discomfort. He mercifully kept his mouth shut until he pulled up in front of the station.

He carried her bag to the train for her and helped her on board.

"Au revoir, mademoiselle," he said, bowing as she climbed the steps into the car. "Safe trip."

Elizabeth smiled gratefully and thanked him for his help. She found her seat and slumped back against the soft cushions, willing herself to relax. *Sweet Valley, here I come,* she thought grimly.

"Elizabeth, will you marry me?"
No, no.
"Elizabeth, will you be my wife?" Laurent's arm slashed the air in frustration. "Elizabeth, will you do me the honor of becoming my wife?" *Better, but not perfect.* He paced the length of his bedroom, trying to think of the perfect words.

Laurent grew tense as he turned over different approaches in his mind. He began to feel suffocated by his jacket and tie and hastily removed them, flinging them aside. He strode the room in a soft white silk shirt, sleeves turned up at the cuffs, and formfitting black pants. Now that he was comfortable, maybe he could think straight.

This is the most important question I will ever ask in my life, he thought helplessly. *The moment must be absolutely perfect.*

He put a hand on either side of his head as if trying to squeeze the right words from his mind. "Why can't I think?" he asked the empty room.

"Laurent!" Pierre burst into his room, shouting his name. "Laurent, you must stop her, you must stop her!"

"Stop who?" he asked. "What is it, Pierre? What are you saying?"

Pierre took a deep breath. "I listened at the door. The countess, she said mean things to Elizabeth." He stopped to try to catch his breath. "She told Elizabeth the country will be in trouble if you don't marry Antonia. There will be an embar . . . an embarge . . ."

"An embargo?" Laurent asked in disbelief.

Pierre nodded. "That's it. And Elizabeth ran away. Please stop her, Laurent!"

Laurent grabbed his little brother by the arm. Suddenly the whole world seemed upside down.

"Where exactly did she go?" he demanded.

Pierre burst into tears at his brother's stern tone of voice. "To the train station," he sobbed. "I heard her tell the driver to hurry."

"It's all right, Pierre." Laurent took a single moment to hug his little brother. "I'm not mad at you. You did the right thing. Now, tell no one else about this," he insisted. He waited to see Pierre nod before he flew out of the room on his way to the stables.

Laurent waved away the help of one of the grooms and ran into Pardaillan's stall. The horse whinnied and stamped his hooves at the familiar footsteps of his master. "Come along, Pardaillan, we have a job to do," Laurent told the stallion as he slid the saddle onto the horse's back and tightened the girth.

"I can't believe she ran away," he told himself while he adjusted the bridle. Pardaillan snorted and shook his head as if he were feeling as angry and anxious as Laurent. The prince led the horse out into the yard, mounted swiftly, and ground his heels against Pardaillan's flanks.

The horse sprang forward, and the wind caught his mane as he galloped across the lawn toward the woods. Laurent's hair flew in the breeze, and his shirt billowed out around him. He felt the strength of the horse beneath him, the sun warm on his back. He dug his heels in a bit more, urging Pardaillan on.

None of this would have happened if it weren't for that horrid countess! I would give anything to get back at her somehow! he thought wildly.

The woods loomed near, and he slowed Pardaillan just a little. They entered the forest, and the stallion picked his way delicately through the roots and across the fallen branches. They splashed through the stream, and Laurent directed the horse over a stray log.

"Easy, Pardaillan," he said to calm the horse after the jump. The big animal sidestepped and almost tripped over a hidden root, and Laurent leaned down and patted his horse reassuringly. "It's all right," he said into the horse's right ear. "Just keep going—we must keep going!"

He heaved a sigh of relief when he saw the edge of the woods ahead. Laurent ducked a low-lying branch, guided Pardaillan around a hole, and burst from the woods at a full gallop.

I hope I am not too late to stop Elizabeth, he thought frantically. *I just can't be too late!*

Chapter 11

Jessica trudged her way through the morning with the children, counting the hours until their nap time. There was no way she could sneak down to the dungeon to see Jacques again until the kids were asleep. When Pierre went off with his mother that morning, Jessica was more than happy to let him go, but that still left Claudine and Manon.

The midday meal consisted of tomato soup and ham and cheese croissants. Jessica giggled to herself. *These princesses eat almost the same thing as American schoolchildren,* she thought. "Claudine, please don't stick your sandwich in Manon's ear," Jessica reprimanded the five-year-old.

"It is to make her laugh," Claudine said in English. Manon was indeed giggling uncontrollably.

"Just don't do it," Jessica said. "And don't dawdle. It's nearly nap time!"

Manon flung half of her croissant to the floor, and Jessica bent to retrieve it.

"Jessica, Jessica," Manon sang as she took the piece of bread from Jessica's hand and immediately threw it back on the floor.

"Manon!" Jessica wailed. "Please don't do this today!" She grabbed up the discarded food and tossed it in a nearby trash can.

"Let's go. It's time for your nap," Jessica said, ushering the girls away from the table.

"Only one story before you lie down. We'll read more tomorrow," Jessica promised as she herded them into the nursery and their waiting beds. As they crawled under the covers she noticed they looked tired, and she smiled in satisfaction. In a few minutes they would be sound asleep and she would be on her way to see Jacques. She read them their story, waited to make sure they were both asleep, and hurried down the steps to the first floor.

All morning she had been formulating a plan. Now, with a little courage, she was ready to act. It was the only way she could think of to help Jacques. And she had to help him. Even after all that had happened, she still loved him.

Jessica stopped at a large, round table in the middle of the huge entrance hall. A beautiful flower arrangement had been placed in the center. Jessica playfully pulled a rose from the blue china vase.

"They'll never miss it," she told herself as she continued on her way. She couldn't wait to see Jacques's face when she gave him the flower.

Finally she reached the dreary corner of the château where a thick wooden door protected the steps leading to the dungeon. She struggled to open the door, marveling at how heavy it was. By the light of a dim bulb she made her way carefully down the uneven, cold stone steps.

At the bottom of the steps Jessica greeted the guard with a smile, thankful that it was the same man who had let her speak to Jacques yesterday. He waved her toward the cell, not even bothering to stand up.

"Jacques?" she called through the bars.

"Jessica! You came yet again!" He stretched his hand through the barred window in the cell door as far as he could reach, and Jessica grasped his fingers in hers. It made her feel sick that she might never again feel his arms around her.

"I have something for you," she said brightly, pushing the bottom end of the rose through the bars. "Since you can't go outside, I brought nature in to you."

He took the rose and sniffed it, his eyes closed in ecstasy. "What a beautiful thing to do, Jessica!" he said. "Thank you."

"I only have a little time," she told him.

Jessica shot a glance at the guard, who was staring blankly at a newspaper. She took a deep breath. It was time to put her plan into action.

"How I wish I could feel your arms around me just once more," Jessica said, raising her voice so she could be sure the guard would hear.

"That would be heaven," Jacques agreed.

"Soon I'll leave for America, and we'll never see each other again!" Jessica wailed dramatically in her best soap opera voice. She noticed the guard looking over at her from the corner of his eye. *I am so good,* she thought.

She smiled slyly at Jacques and then pulled away from the door.

"Jessica," Jacques hissed. "What are you doing?"

Jessica approached the guard slowly.

"Could you do something for me?" she asked in her sweetest, most innocent voice.

"Depends on what it is," the young man said, his eyes suddenly wary.

"It's just . . . ," Jessica began, willing tears to form in her eyes. "It's just that . . ."

The guard waited expectantly.

"It's just that I love him so much!" she wailed, bursting into uncontrollable sobs.

The guard jumped back a little, startled by her sudden outburst.

"I need to feel his arms around me one more time," she cried, reaching out and clutching his shirt. "Please, please let me into the cell. I'm never going to see him again!"

The guard shook his head and removed her hands from his arm.

"That I cannot do, mademoiselle. I would lose my job if someone found out," he told her, his voice firm but kind.

"Oh, but I wouldn't tell anyone," she said, wiping at her eyes. "If you did this for me, I would be so grateful. I would never forget your kindness."

She flashed him a hopeful smile, tears still streaming down her face.

The guard hesitated, obviously wanting to grant her request but still worried about the consequences. For a moment Jessica thought her plan had failed. Then he finally smiled.

"I think you are more French than American, mademoiselle," he said with a shake of his head. "So much passion and emotion in such a little girl."

He got up and chose the correct key from the ring of keys he wore at his belt.

"Thank you," Jessica gushed, impulsively reaching up to kiss the guard lightly on the cheek.

The guard blushed again and touched his cheek. They walked over to Jacques's cell together.

"I will have to lock the door behind you, mademoiselle," he said, turning the key in the lock.

"I understand," Jessica agreed, nearly jumping out of her skin with excitement. In a moment Jacques would be free!

As soon as the cell door was open she threw herself against the guard with all her strength.

"Run, Jacques, run!" she screamed.

The guard was so surprised by Jessica's action that he fell to the floor off-balance, and Jessica tumbled on top of him. The guard sprawled and struggled beneath her as Jacques sprinted from the cell down the short hallway and up the dungeon stairs.

"What are you doing?" the guard screamed in French. "Get up now!" Jessica rose slowly, taking her time to give Jacques a better chance.

Jessica smiled to herself at her success, not even minding that the guard was spewing French at her in an angry voice as he tried to get to his feet. When he began to follow Jacques, Jessica stuck out her foot, and the guard went down again with a thud. She skipped to the side to avoid the guard's grasping hand and ran toward the door.

Just as she reached the bottom of the stairs she heard a scuffling noise on the stairway. She looked up to find Jacques, almost suspended off the ground, between two other guards.

"Jacques!" she cried, her hand flying to her throat in shock.

"Sorry, *ma chérie*," he said sadly. "Thank you for trying."

They dragged Jacques down the stairs, and Jessica reached out to him as they passed. Jacques tried to grab her hand, but the guards yanked him away. They threw Jacques back into the cell and slammed the door the door shut with an eerie thud.

Jessica was too shocked to move. Jacques had come so close to freedom.

One of the new guards stomped over to base of the stairs, where Jessica was still standing.

"If I see you down here again," he spat in a guttural voice, bringing his face within inches of hers, "I will lock you up too!"

Jessica fled the dungeon with fresh tears of real pain streaming down her cheeks.

Elizabeth sat on the train, wondering when it would finally get going. She almost believed she could feel her heart actually breaking inside her. She missed Laurent desperately, and knowing she would never set eyes on him again made that much worse.

The quicker she got to Paris, the quicker she could get on a flight home and put this summer behind her. That was all she wanted now, the comfort of her parents and friends, of her own world.

Jessica will probably kill me for leaving her alone with the kids for the rest of the summer, she thought. Elizabeth's heart ached for her sister too. Jacques was in the dungeon with no hope of being released, and Elizabeth knew that Jessica felt as horrible as she did. How did everything go so wrong?

Nothing has ever hurt this bad, she thought, shifting in her seat as if changing position would ease the pain she felt.

"I'm really never going to see him again," she said to herself, as if saying the words out loud would help her accept the reality they described. *Why is doing the right thing always so unbelievably hard?* she wondered.

The train gave a sudden lurch. *Thank goodness we're on our way,* Elizabeth thought. She turned her head to look out the window at the passing scenery. Suddenly she saw a man on horseback barreling toward the train at top speed. *What kind of idiot would ride a horse up next to a train?* Elizabeth asked herself. *Isn't that kind of dangerous?*

But as the rider came closer, Elizabeth's eyes widened in surprise. She would know those broad shoulders and that thick black hair anywhere.

It was Laurent. And he was guiding Pardaillan next to the moving train!

Elizabeth's heart jumped into her throat, and she wondered if she were dreaming.

No, she thought suddenly. *He's really here! He came! He came for me!*

Elizabeth held her breath at the sight of him, galloping up to the train on Pardaillan. He looked so strong and unbelievably handsome. Elizabeth half stood as her heart pounded up into her ears. Laurent spotted her through the window.

"I love you, Elizabeth!" he shouted. His hair whipped back from his face as he leaned forward in the saddle, trying to pick up speed.

Pardaillan moved forward to the door of the car, and Elizabeth pressed her face against the window so she could see Laurent leap from the saddle and through the door. Her joyful tears left streaks on the glass. She whirled around to see him enter the car, tall and commanding.

"Stop this train at once!" he ordered the conductor.

The other passengers were all talking excitedly in mingled English and French. "It is the prince!" "Prince Laurent has stopped the train!" "He is more handsome than his picture!"

Elizabeth was barely conscious of those snippets of conversation as Laurent strode toward her.

He had never looked so handsome or sexy. His dark hair was ruffled after his wild ride, and the cuffs of his white shirt were rolled up, exposing his strong, tanned arms. He looked more like a prince at that moment than he had in any uniform she had seen him in.

"Laurent," she whispered joyfully. She could hardly believe he was there.

Laurent reached over and swept her up in his arms. He looked deeply into her eyes, and she went dizzy with the intensity. Before she knew what was happening, he was kissing her passionately, and she tightened her arms around him to keep from buckling under the force of her own overwhelming emotion. She had never loved anyone as much as she loved Laurent at that moment.

When they finally drew apart, Elizabeth slowly realized that the people in the car were cheering wildly and waving their arms. Elizabeth felt herself blush furiously at the thought that all these people had watched her and Laurent kissing.

But she couldn't stay embarrassed for long. Nothing mattered as long as she was with Laurent.

He clasped her hands in his.

"Oh, Laurent," she said, almost afraid to look into his blazing blue eyes again.

"You were crazy to leave like this, Elizabeth," Laurent began in mock sternness. "I don't care if it does cause a war; I won't marry Antonia. I can't stand the sight of her. Because of you I know what true love really is. And I refuse to settle for less." Laurent knelt before her, right there in the aisle. "Elizabeth, please marry me."

Elizabeth gasped, hardly daring to believe all he had just said.

"What . . . but . . . ," she stuttered.

Laurent stood up and put his finger gently to her trembling lips.

"Don't answer right away," he said quickly. "Just promise me you'll think about it." Elizabeth could only nod, she was so overwhelmed.

As Laurent took her in his arms again Elizabeth lost control of her emotions. She laughed through tears of joy and buried her face in the front of his soft silk shirt.

Laurent kept one arm securely around

Elizabeth's shoulders as they made their way down the aisle to the door.

"Please have Miss Wakefield's luggage sent to the château at once," he asked the conductor.

"Of course, Your Grace," the conductor answered quickly, saluting.

The passengers were still clapping and cheering as Elizabeth stepped from the train. Outside, a man was holding Pardaillan's bridle.

"Here, Your Grace, I have kept your horse for you," the man said in French.

"Merci beaucoup," Laurent replied. He turned to Elizabeth and effortlessly lifted her onto the front of the saddle. Then he climbed on behind her and wrapped one arm securely around her waist. She leaned back into the embrace, feeling totally secure and blissfully happy. As they rode off toward the château Elizabeth's ears still rang with the cheers of the passengers. She was living the fairy tale; she only hoped it would end happily ever after!

Jessica waited in the darkness of her room, her door slightly ajar, wishing Laurent would finally let Elizabeth go in to bed. She desperately needed to talk to the prince about Jacques, but she didn't want to disturb the happy couple.

They were sharing a lingering kiss in front of the door to the room, and the way Laurent caressed Elizabeth's cheek made Jessica's heart melt.

Good for you, Liz! she thought. Her very own sister had snatched a prince out of the grasp of that horrid Antonia di Rimini.

At least one of us ended up with royalty, she thought. She remembered that when they started this trip, she herself had dreamed of a romance with a handsome noble. She'd even thought she'd snagged herself a future duke when she met Jacques. But she wouldn't change places with Elizabeth. Jacques might not be what she'd thought he was, but that didn't make her love him any less.

At long last Elizabeth opened her door and went into her room. Laurent let out a deep, satisfied sigh and turned to leave.

"Laurent," Jessica hissed from the shadows.

Laurent spun around, his expression startled.

"Who's there?" he asked quickly, then saw her face. "Jessica, why are you hiding?"

Jessica clasped her hands tightly together to keep them from trembling.

"I have to talk to you, but I didn't want to bother you and Elizabeth when . . . well, you know," she said, and gestured toward Elizabeth's closed door.

Laurent smiled slightly and nodded his understanding. "What can I do for you?" he asked.

"I need your help, Laurent," she explained. "Where can we talk privately?"

"This way," he said, and led her down the stairs

of the tower and into a small sitting room. Shelves of leather-bound books lined the walls. It smelled musty, as if it wasn't used very often. But when Laurent lit the lamp, the room immediately became warm and cozy.

"Is this private enough, Jessica?" he asked kindly.

"Oh, yes, thank you," she said, feeling much more hopeful now that Laurent was being so cooperative.

They sat down on soft, comfortable red damask chairs on either side of the big stone fireplace. "Would you like me to have a fire built?" Laurent asked. "These unused rooms can be cold even in the summertime."

"No, thank you," she said, warmed by his kindness. She took a deep breath. "It's about Jacques, Laurent. Is there anything you can do to help him? All he wants is to return the things he stole and try to make an honest living." Jessica tried to keep her emotions under control, knowing hysterics probably wouldn't work on the levelheaded prince.

Laurent leaned forward with real concern in his warm blue eyes. Jessica could understand why Elizabeth had fallen so hard for him; he positively radiated compassion.

"Jessica, in this case my hands are tied," he told her plainly and quietly. "It is bad enough that I caused trouble by refusing to marry the woman my father chose for me. That's enough of an international mess."

"What do you mean, 'international mess'?" Jessica asked. She had been so wrapped up in her concern for Jacques, she had missed the scandal that the countess's threats had caused.

"The countess tried to drive Elizabeth away by making her feel guilty about my decision. She even said there might be a trade war if I don't marry Antonia," he explained.

"But you broke up with her anyway?" Jessica asked, amazed. She hadn't known Elizabeth could have such power over men.

"Yes," Laurent answered wearily. "But my father is an accomplished diplomat. I believe he will find a way to appease the countess."

Laurent raked an impatient hand through his thick, dark hair. "But as for what you ask . . . Jacques's crime was too great. I do not know if my father could fix the present situation if he also refused to prosecute the thief who stole the countess's jewels."

"But he's willing to return them!" Jessica cried. "Do you think she might agree to let him go if she got her crummy jewelry back?"

"I doubt it," Laurent answered, touching her shoulder in sympathy. "She has never been reasonable about anything else."

The tears overflowed her eyes and cascaded down her cheeks, and Jessica made no effort to wipe them away. "I wish I had never even heard of the Château d'Amour Inconnu," she wailed, covering her face with her hands.

"Jessica, please don't cry," Laurent said in a pained voice. "Here, take my handkerchief."

Jessica groped for the soft cloth and held it to her eyes, despair overwhelming her heart.

"Poor Jacques," she said through her tears.

"Jessica," Laurent said decisively, "if I see the opportunity to help Jacques, I will. I promise. There's no telling, of course, if it will be possible. But I give you my solemn oath, on my honor, that I will try."

Jessica smiled at him through her tears.

"Thank you, Laurent!" she said quietly. "Just knowing that you'll try to help makes me feel much better." She sniffled and dabbed at her eyes, wondering if she dared hope that Jacques might after all be set free.

But she could only hope and wait, and that had to be the hardest thing of all.

Chapter 12

Elizabeth sat down in front of the mirror and smoothed a bit of moisturizer over her face. She looked at her lips, still warm from Laurent's kiss. Having Laurent whisk her away from the train like that was the most romantic thing that had ever happened to her. No one had ever made her feel so cherished.

And that proposal! Prince Laurent actually wanted to marry her. She pinched herself for the hundredth time to make sure she wasn't dreaming. What if she said yes? What would it be like to be a real princess?

For a moment Elizabeth let herself daydream about the possibilities. Her picture would appear in every newspaper and magazine in the world. She would attend balls and receptions in honor of her engagement to Laurent. And after the wedding they would travel to different countries all over the world.

"The things I would learn!" she said in awe. "International politics, new languages . . . I would be speaking perfect French in no time."

Elizabeth placed the jar of moisturizer on top of her bureau and walked over to the window. Outside, moonlight bathed the lawn in shimmering silver light. It truly looked like something out of a fairy tale. Would she be spending her future in this wonderful place?

If she agreed to marry Laurent, their years would be divided between Paris and the château. They would spend their summers here, riding and swimming with their children. In time Laurent would assume the throne, and Elizabeth would be at his side, his partner and his love.

Elizabeth could see herself, sitting beside a roaring fire, two little children playing at her feet. One of them might be a darkly handsome little boy, toddling about, grasping at her knee to steady himself. And maybe, playing on the carpet with a baby doll, a blond little girl, singing softly.

The travel would be the best, she thought. *Laurent and I could walk along the banks of the Seine and discuss philosophy and literature. We might even read poetry together!*

She turned away from the window and sat down on her narrow bed, tucking one foot beneath her. *What exactly does a princess do with her days?* she wondered thoughtfully.

"Let's see," she said out loud, organizing her thoughts, "the royal family in England does a lot of charity work and fund-raising."

That would be great, but what about a career? She could hardly pursue a conventional writing career as a princess.

"Of course," she continued out loud, "everything I wrote would sell!" For a moment her heart soared at the thought of such success.

But then a new thought deflated her.

"That would hardly be fulfilling. I want my writing to be published because it's good, not because I'm some kind of celebrity." She leaned back against the headboard and folded her knees up under her chin, hugging them with her arms.

"What am I doing?" she asked herself harshly. She was actually considering accepting Laurent's proposal! It hadn't been long since she believed she and Todd would be together forever.

Suddenly her eye caught sight of the cover of her journal on the desk. She jumped off the bed to retrieve it, then sat in the chair by the window. She flipped through the pages absently, reading little snippets as she went. There were the names of all her friends—Enid, Maria, Winston . . . Todd.

What if she did just go back to Sweet Valley and pick up her life where it left off? What was really left back there anyway? Todd had made his desires perfectly clear. . . . They were free to see other people. Elizabeth couldn't believe it actually still hurt to think about that last night with Todd!

Was it that they had such a history together? Elizabeth and Todd had known each other since they were kids. And Elizabeth couldn't remember a time when she hadn't loved him. *We have had our ups and downs,* she thought. *But no matter what has happened, we always end up together in the end.* Could it ever be the same with Todd again?

If she said yes to Prince Laurent, her relationship with Todd would obviously be over, but what about everyone else? What would her friends and family say if Jessica came home without her? Would they believe that levelheaded, down-to-earth Elizabeth could have her head turned by a prince?

She closed the journal abruptly, put it back in its place on the desk, and flopped into bed. Pulling the covers up to her chin, she stared at the ceiling, her mind unquiet.

The one thing Elizabeth had no doubt about was her own feelings for Laurent. She did love him. But she also found herself longing for Todd and the security of home. Laurent excited her in a way no boy ever had, but Todd was still such a huge part of her life. Elizabeth knew she would never sleep that night.

What am I going to do?

❖ ❖ ❖

Laurent woke up with a strong white light shining in his eyes. He instinctively put a hand in front of his face.

"Who are you, and what are you doing in my room?" he demanded.

"Shhh," said a strange voice as the light was directed across the room. "I will not harm you."

"How did you get in here? Answer me, or I'll call the guards!" Laurent moved for the lamp on his bedside table and turned it on. An older man with graying hair and soft blue eyes was standing beside his bed, dressed completely in black.

"No need for that, sir," the man said quietly.

"Then tell me who you are!" Laurent thundered. "I can have you thrown into the dungeon for entering this room uninvited in the middle of the night!"

"Sir, I beg you, please keep your voice down. There is no need to alert anyone to my presence here." The older man backed up a step, and Laurent felt better. He got out of bed and tied a robe around his waist. Being on his feet made him feel more in control of the situation.

"Unless you tell me right this instant who you are and what business you have here, the whole château will be alerted," Laurent said in a quieter but no less demanding voice.

"My name is Louis Savant," the man began. "I am the father of Jacques Savant, the young man you have in your dungeon. I am the real thief, sir."

Laurent was surprised but not at all frightened. Now that he had the chance to look the man up and down, he could see that everything about him seemed to be gentle and nonviolent. He stood there so quietly, hands at his sides, shoulders relaxed. The love Louis felt for his son was obvious, shining like a beacon in his eyes.

"Why have you come here?" Laurent asked again, but this time more kindly.

"Will you listen to what I have to say?" the man asked in his cultured French. "I mean, really listen?"

"Of course. Provided what you tell me is the truth," Laurent said, trying to sound firm but fair.

"I am not a liar," Louis protested.

"But you are a jewel thief," Laurent pointed out. "Some people might have a hard time believing your version of any truth."

"Agreed," Louis said. "But I swear to you on my son's life that I will be honest."

Laurent gestured to two chairs in the corner of his room. The older man sat and crossed his legs comfortably. He looked as if he would be at home anywhere from a waterfront tavern to the ballroom of a king. Laurent found himself warming to the older man in spite of himself.

"I am listening," he said to Louis, crossing his own legs and placing his arms on the chair's armrests in a posture of complete attention.

"Many years ago," Louis began, his voice a little

wistful, "I owned a grocery shop in Paris. I sold the finest vegetables in the city. Great chefs would buy from no one else for their fancy restaurants." He began to cough, leaning forward in his chair, his hand cupped before his mouth.

"Would you like some water?" Laurent offered. The cough sounded chronic and quite serious.

Mr. Savant shook his head no, and when the coughing subsided, he continued.

"My wife was a very fine seamstress, and together we made enough to live comfortably. Not extravagantly. We had Jacques and each other, and we wanted nothing more."

Laurent was puzzled. "It's a huge leap from the kind of life you're describing to a life of crime."

"Yes," Mr. Savant said, nodding to emphasize his words. "When Jacques was ten years old, my wife became ill, there was no money for her expensive medicines, and she died. I suppose . . . I suppose a piece of me died with her. There I was, left with Jacques, but I had no more desire to work or even to live."

"I'm sorry your wife died," Laurent said with real sympathy. "But many people lose loved ones. They don't all begin stealing jewels as a result."

Mr. Savant shook his head sadly.

"I was very angry and bitterly hurt," he explained. "You see, I applied to my wife's customers for help paying for the medicine. I would have paid them back in time, but no." His voice turned harsh. "While she was well, they would have no one else make their fancy dresses. But they had no feeling for her when she was helplessly dying."

"We all do things we regret when we are angry or hurt," Laurent admitted. "But why bring Jacques into it? Surely it was unwise to teach a young boy to steal!"

Mr. Savant smiled. "Jacques was a reluctant thief at the best of times. He has been after me for some years to retire."

"I'm still not sure what reason you have for coming here tonight," Laurent said, although he was beginning to suspect one.

"I make no excuses for myself," Mr. Savant said firmly, sitting straighter in his chair. "I made my choices, and now I am willing to pay for my crimes. If you will just release my son, you can take me in his place. My life has nearly run its course. He has all his life before him."

"But why come to me?" Laurent insisted. "It is my father who has the power to release Jacques."

"Your father is a man known for his fairness and generosity," Mr. Savant said carefully. "But he is also a political leader. I don't believe he can extend such mercy without losing his standing in the international community."

Laurent was amused at how well Mr. Savant avoided criticizing his father. He realized he didn't want to see this man rot in prison for the rest of his life. He was too charming and too kind. And if

what he said about Jacques was true, he didn't deserve to be locked away either.

Suddenly a thought occurred to him.

If Jacques and his father both disappeared, the
countess would be cheated of her revenge. *What a
perfect way to pay her back for what she did to
Elizabeth!* Laurent thought.

The prince reached out and grasped the older
man's hand.

"I understand how great your loss has been and
how much your son means to you. If the guard in
the dungeon had to leave . . ."

"Yes, Prince Laurent?" Mr. Savant asked eagerly.

"If there happened to be a trespasser, and I told the
guard to check the front lawn, that would leave your
son unattended," Laurent said in a conspiratorial voice.

"And if Jacques is unguarded, he might escape," Mr. Savant prompted.

"With a little help," Laurent assured him
quickly. "There is a spare set of keys on the kitchen
wall downstairs. Here," he said, opening a drawer
in his desk, "you will need some money to get
away." He handed Louis a few bills.

"What an extraordinary young man you are,"
Mr. Savant said warmly. When Laurent reached
out to clasp Louis's hand, he felt something small
and jagged press against his fingers. He pulled his
hand away to find the diamond necklace resting in
his palm.

"You have earned my eternal gratitude," Louis said.

The two men slipped from Laurent's room in silence, ready to put their plan into action.

Jacques thought he was dreaming when he heard someone call his name. He awoke slowly, his eyes struggling to adjust to the pitch-darkness. He heard the scrape of metal on metal and wondered what was going on.

"Hello?" he called softly. Could the guard be coming in here for some reason?

It seemed like only a moment ago that the man had told him it was time to turn out the light and go to sleep. Engulfed by darkness, Jacques had no choice but to lie on the cot and lose himself in his miserable thoughts. But eventually sleep came and with it dreams of Jessica, her shimmering golden hair and startling blue-green eyes, the way she touched his arm when she talked. It hurt so badly to think they would be apart forever.

Now Jacques sat up on the cot and could just make out the figure of a person on the other side of the barred window in the cell door.

"Who's there? What are you doing?" he called softly.

Jacques stood up in his cell. Who was on the other side of that door? Could it be Jessica coming to release him in the dead of night? Or perhaps the guards had been ordered to take him somewhere else. He wished his eyes would adjust to the darkness.

After more scraping the cell door swung open and a voice whispered, "Jacques, are you there?"

Jacques would have known that voice anywhere.

"Papa!" he whispered into the darkness, clasping the older man to his chest. "But how . . . why . . ."

"Shhh, my son. You did not think I would let you rot in this dungeon, did you?" The old man sounded as cheerful as ever, as if they weren't both in danger of going to prison for the rest of their lives.

"How did you find out I was here?" Jacques asked hoarsely. He couldn't help hanging on to his father. He had thought he would never see him again.

"You know I have my ways," the older man replied, patting Jacques's hand, which was on his arm. "At least now I know you have not been harmed. I have been crazed with worry for you!"

"I'm all right, Papa," Jacques answered, tears in his eyes. "Especially now. I thought you were gone forever."

"Jacques, I must tell you something," Louis said, for once sounding very serious. "I vow to you we will never steal again."

"But Papa," Jacques said, "what made you decide this? I have been hoping for years, but—"

"When I learned you were in the dungeon,"

Louis interrupted, "I thought I would die. The thought of you sitting in this cell . . . it changed my mind about everything."

Jacques hugged his father again.

"Oh, Papa, I am so happy," he cried. "We will go somewhere warm, where you will feel better and get completely well again. I will work very hard."

"We both will," Louis said. "We will do this together, son." Louis glanced back nervously at the dungeon door. "Let us go. We dare not delay."

Jacques put a restraining hand on his father's arm.

"Wait. I must leave a note for Jessica. I need to say good-bye."

The older man sighed impatiently. "The American girl again? Why are you so taken with her?"

"I don't know, Papa," Jacques said, equally impatient. "I only know it would be terrible to escape without letting her know I am all right."

"Ah, Jacques," Louis said with a sigh. "You are truly my son to insist on this. Nothing gets in the way of romance."

Jacques rummaged through the desk where the guard sat and found paper and a pencil. He began to scribble a hasty note. His father watched over his shoulder.

"Papa, I can't think with you standing right there," Jacques complained.

"You should say something about the moonlight and her eyes," Louis offered in a dreamy voice.

"Don't worry, Papa," Jacques assured him with a smile. The old man was a hopeless romantic. "I know exactly what to say."

He wrote Jessica's name on the outside of the folded paper and left it on his cot. In a last sentimental moment he kissed the tips of his fingers and touched the paper with them. "Good-bye, beautiful Jessica," he whispered.

At the top of the stairs, with freedom a few steps away, Jacques put his hand on his father's arm.

"Papa, tell me truthfully," he said. "You have not hurt anyone in order to get me out, have you?"

"Your release is the gift of a very kind and compassionate young man," his father explained.

Jacques could think of only one young man who could have done this. Somehow his father had persuaded Prince Laurent to help them escape. Why else would the guard have left his post? How else could his father have obtained a key to his cell?

Jacques's opinion of the prince changed completely. Maybe he wasn't such a spoiled, pampered young man. Maybe there was some substance to him after all. Jacques and his father were now in Laurent's debt. And Jacques silently vowed that someday he would repay the prince's kindness.

Chapter 13

The next morning Jessica thought she would never get her makeup right. She was so distraught over Jacques that she barely slept a wink, and her eyes were puffy and would look terrible if she wasn't careful. She expertly applied the palest blue eye shadow, followed by a few swipes of mascara.

"Perfect!" she said to her reflection, smiling in satisfaction.

She picked up her brush and combed her hair until it gleamed.

I'm not exactly looking forward to fighting past the guards this morning after what happened yesterday, she thought. *But I just have to do it. Jacques needs all my support.*

She stepped backward to admire herself further. She was wearing a stylish white sundress with spaghetti straps that made her blond hair even more brilliant than usual. Low-heeled white sandals completed the outfit, making her look positively angelic.

"Jacques has no one else in the world but me," she said out loud, her heart giving a painful lurch. Jacques's father seemed to have vanished into thin air. Did he even know his son was in the dungeon at the château?

Jessica remembered that the note Jacques's father had left at the inn had mentioned some friends he was meeting. So it was entirely possible he didn't know about Jacques's arrest. But would he risk coming here even if he did?

"Right now it doesn't matter," she told herself. "Until his father shows up, I have to support Jacques. I have to get in to see him."

She left her room resolutely and walked down the tower steps, wondering how she could persuade the guards to let her see Jacques.

She walked quickly through the corridors of the château. The paintings of Laurent's ancestors scowled down on her from the walls, and she stuck out her tongue at one particularly snobbish-looking woman.

Maybe if I pretend to be Elizabeth, they'll let me in! Jessica thought as she hurried along. *Those stupid guards couldn't possibly tell us apart!*

Jessica had begun forming her plan when she halted in surprise. The door to the dungeon steps was standing wide open. She picked down the stairs. There was no guard. What luck!

Jessica stepped carefully down the uneven, cold stone steps, wrinkling her nose in distaste at the familiar, musty smell. It couldn't be healthy to stay in this cold, clammy place for very long. Jacques had to get out of here!

When she reached the bottom of the stairs, Jessica realized that the door to Jacques's cell was open as well. *Where is he?* she thought frantically. *Did they take him to some other cell? Or did they take him directly to prison? I should have stayed here all last night!*

There was something on Jacques's abandoned cot, something white and square. A piece of paper. She entered the cell and sat on the cot, snatching up the paper and realizing her name was written on it. With trembling hands Jessica unfolded the note.

Dear Jessica,

I will always love you. For now I must go away, but I promise you we will meet again. Never forget me, for I will never forget the beautiful American who stole my heart the way I used to steal gems.

Jacques

Jessica felt a wave of relief wash over her like the waves from the Pacific Ocean at home. She held the note up against her wildly beating heart, wishing Jacques could know how much she loved him and how happy she was that he had gotten away.

Oh, Jacques, she thought as tears of joy stung her eyes, *please be safe! Maybe someday we can be together again!*

"Mademoiselle Jessica?" a small voice said.

Jessica started and looked up to see Manon in the doorway of the cell.

"Manon, have you been following me?" Jessica demanded.

Manon's only answer was to stretch out her pudgy little arms, imploring Jessica to pick her up. Jessica couldn't help smiling, and she stood and went to the little girl. She lifted Manon into her arms and hugged her, then sat back down on the cot with the child on her lap.

"What are you doing here?" Jessica asked.

Manon shrugged, then said carefully in English, "I do not know."

"I don't know either," Jessica said frankly.

"What is it?" Manon asked, pointing to the paper, which Jessica still held in her hand.

"This?" Jessica said. "Nothing you need to worry about for a long time." Suddenly she felt chilled. This was no place for a small child. "Let's get out of here. It's cold."

Jessica stood and put Manon down. Then she folded the note twice, creasing it very carefully, and shoved it deep into the one pocket in her dress. She would keep the note for the rest of her life as proof that she had known and loved a handsome French thief named Jacques Savant.

* * *

"What do you intend to do about the escape of that rapscallion jewel thief?" the countess demanded of the prince and princess, flushing an unnaturally dark shade of red. Laurent wondered if she would soon just blow up, like an overheated balloon.

The older prince took a deep breath.

"We are not even sure of his name, let alone where he may have run to," he said in his most diplomatic voice.

"You should have every guard combing the countryside," the countess continued shrilly.

"They have been searching the grounds since the escape was discovered at dawn," the prince said wearily. Laurent could see the countess was beginning to wear on his father.

"Countess," the princess interjected, "you must not worry yourself over these matters. Please allow my husband to take care of the search for the thief and of his ultimate fate, if we find him. You have your jewels back; what more do you wish?"

"I demand justice!" the countess thundered, almost purple with rage. "Don't you think I know how that boy escaped? It was those horrible au pairs. Those American brats!"

Laurent couldn't let the conversation go on this way.

"No, Countess," he interjected, straining to be

polite. "I can assure you Jessica and Elizabeth had nothing to do with the escape."

"Yes," his father said quickly. "We considered they might be tempted to try to help their friend again, so I had a guard stationed outside their rooms all night. They never left the tower."

"I don't believe it," the countess huffed.

For the first time in dealing with her, Laurent's father looked angry.

"Are you saying you doubt my word and that of my son?" The prince began to drum his fingers on a nearby tabletop, a sure sign that he was about to lose his temper.

Laurent couldn't tell whether the countess was insensitive to the warning in his father's voice or simply too angry to care.

"Your son has been stubborn and disobedient, not to mention disrespectful. Why should I believe anything he says? As for you . . ."

Laurent saw his stepmother go pale and his father's face turn the slightest shade of red.

"Countess, I believe that there are matters in Italy that demand your attention," he said, his tone formal and firm. "I am so sorry you will have to cut your visit short, but I understand that duty calls."

"You are asking me to leave the château?" the countess sputtered. "You are throwing me out?"

"Whatever interpretation you choose," Laurent's father continued. "I am certain you will be happier away from my family and away from France."

"Well," the countess said, squaring her shoulders and taking a deep breath. "It is certainly fortunate our royal houses will not be joined."

"I assure you," Laurent's stepmother said with a smile, "the good fortune is entirely ours." Laurent smothered a laugh as the countess flounced from the room. He hugged each of his parents. "Thank you," he said, his spirit light.

The prince and his stepmother smiled at him.

"Go find your beautiful American, Laurent. Be happy," his father said.

Laurent's heart soared with happiness and love as he turned and hurried from the room. It was time to see Elizabeth!

Elizabeth and Laurent walked across the lawn, hand in hand, just before lunch. The sun was warm and comforting, and the salty sea breeze ruffled Elizabeth's hair gently. The perfectly manicured lawn was a soft carpet beneath her feet, and the château shimmered in the distance like a fairy castle. Her ankle felt better after a few days' rest. In fact, she hardly felt any pain at all.

Elizabeth was content, walking with her prince. But she was also nervous about giving him an answer to his proposal, so she tried to keep the conversation as light as possible.

"Jessica came back from her visit this morning and said Jacques was gone," she began. "Did you have something to do with that?"

Laurent's warm blue eyes sparkled with mischief.

"Elizabeth, some secrets are better left as secrets," he said knowingly. She could tell he was at the bottom of Jacques's escape, and she was grateful. Her impression had always been that Laurent was a fine and noble person. Why had she ever doubted him?

"I thought I saw the countess and Antonia leaving the château this morning. Have they returned to Italy?" she asked, hoping desperately that they were out of her hair forever.

"Oh, yes," Laurent replied, laughing. "And you should have seen the state the countess was in."

"She's always in a state about something," Elizabeth said, rolling her eyes. "What was it this time?"

"She accused you and Jessica of helping Jacques to escape," Laurent explained. "And when I stood up for you, she accused me of being a liar. So my father suggested she might be happier in Italy, and she practically exploded!"

"Oh, no," Elizabeth cried, bursting into laughter. "Your father actually threw them out?"

"I think he would say he reminded them of where they actually belong," Laurent said, still grinning.

She sobered a moment later, though, as she considered Laurent's parents. "How do your parents really feel about your decision not to marry Antonia?" Elizabeth asked, genuinely concerned.

"I was surprised at their reaction," Laurent said. "They're making a real effort to understand how I feel. They told me it's time to make a change in our traditions."

"That sounds encouraging," she said. "I always thought your parents were nice. It must be hard to up-hold family traditions, sit at the head of a country, and raise a family, all at the same time." She wasn't just talking about Laurent's parents. She was thinking what it would mean if she was faced with that kind of future.

"I've never been sure how they kept it all to-gether," Laurent admitted. "I suppose I never gave it a lot of thought."

They stopped walking when they reached the edge of the pond, which reflected the sunlight and brightened the day even more. The long, wild grasses that grew just at the water's edge bent gently in the breeze. Elizabeth settled on the grass, patting it with her hand.

"Let's sit here," she suggested.

"What a perfect day!" Laurent said, taking a deep breath of the tangy air.

"Do you remember the first time we came here?" she asked. "I thought it must be the most beautiful place on the whole island."

"It is," he said, "and also my favorite spot to daydream. It's where I first saw the beautiful blond girl who later came into my life."

"We have managed to make some wonderful memories, haven't we?" she said. "The dinner on the beach, even the dance the night of the ball . . . I'll remember all of it, always."

As they sat beside the pond in comfortable silence Elizabeth knew the moment of truth was close at hand. She would have to give her answer to Laurent, and part of her was still undecided. The water glistened in the sunlight, rippling ever so slightly. The trees surrounded them on the outer edge of the lawn, like silent sentries. Even the birds' songs seemed to have a hushed quality about them.

Laurent took her hand in his and lifted it to his lips, kissing it ever so gently.

"Elizabeth, we should talk," he whispered against her hand, looking up at her with his beautiful blue eyes shining.

"Yes, I know," she answered quietly.

"Have you considered my proposal?" he asked.

"Yes, very carefully," she said, thinking of the hours she had spent turning the question over and over in her mind. She looked into his eyes and almost changed her mind again. But she couldn't do that and be true to herself.

She took a deep breath and spoke. "Laurent, I truly love you more than anything in this world, and I believe we could be happy together. But I have a whole other life back in Sweet Valley."

"I know that," Laurent said quietly.

"I have family and friends that I care about. My sister is going home soon, and we've hardly ever been separated since the day we were born," she said, feeling the tears just behind her eyes.

"What are you saying, Elizabeth?" Laurent asked, his eyes suddenly clouding over.

Elizabeth took both of his hands into hers and kissed him deeply, with all the love she felt in her heart. When she pulled away, her heart felt heavy.

"I can't marry you, Laurent."

Laurent was crushed by Elizabeth's words. He had been so sure she would say yes!

"But the way we love each other, Elizabeth," he pleaded, "it is for life!"

Tears welled in the corners of her eyes. "I know, I feel that way too, but—"

"No 'buts,'" he said quickly. "I cannot bear the thought of a life without you by my side!"

"Laurent, please," she said, trying to wipe away her tears with her hands. "We're both so young, we have our whole lives ahead of us. Maybe we will end up together, just not right now."

Laurent leaped up from the grass and paced back and forth. "But I want you now!" he cried, not caring how desperate he sounded. "My parents expect me to marry soon, and I won't marry anyone but you!" He jerked his handkerchief from his pocket and handed it to her. It hurt him to see her crying, but he also couldn't bear the thought of life without her.

"Marriage is such a big step," Elizabeth went on, her voice pleading and reasonable. "I can't just rush into it, even loving you the way I do."

"What can I say to persuade you?" he said wildly. "A long engagement? You could go back to Sweet Valley to break it gently to your parents." Elizabeth just shook her head, and Laurent raked a hand through his hair in desperation. "Tell me what I can do to make you say yes."

"Nothing," she said softly. "Please, Laurent, forgive me for hurting you, but I can't say yes, not right now."

Her gentle, quietly spoken words somehow calmed him. She sat there on the grass, dabbing at her eyes with his handkerchief, her shoulders trembling with silent sobs. His heart felt too large for his chest, and there were tears behind his eyes.

"There is nothing to forgive," he said, and his voice was hoarse with unshed tears.

Elizabeth looked up at him, her blue-green eyes watery and yet more beautiful than he had ever seen them.

"Thank you," she whispered.

Laurent sank back onto the grass, feeling more defeated than if he had just fought a great battle.

"I can't force you to marry me," he said in a softer voice. "It's just that I love you so much. I feel for you what I always thought I should feel for the girl I would marry."

"I feel the same way," Elizabeth said, and she

seemed to be recovering herself. She wiped the corners of her eyes one last time, then held the handkerchief in her lap.

Laurent reached up and pushed a strand of her golden hair back in place.

"Thank you," he said, looking deep into her eyes. "To know that you love me as much as I love you is something I will hold in my heart always."

Elizabeth smiled. "Whoever you marry will be a truly lucky girl. You will be a wonderful husband, Laurent," she said, reaching out to hold his hand.

"Someday," he said and took her hand. "Perhaps you are right, we are too young. If my parents allow me to pick my bride, they should also allow me to marry at whatever age I feel ready."

"Good for you," Elizabeth said encouragingly.

"What do you think our future will really be, Elizabeth?"

"Together?" she teased gently. It was good to see her smile, even if it was a rather watery smile.

"Together, apart, tell me what you think," he coaxed. He put his arms around her, and she leaned in against him.

"I want to pursue a writing career, but I'm not sure whether I want to try for newspapers or magazines," she said thoughtfully. "I almost had a summer job working for a magazine before Jessica persuaded me to come here."

"Are you glad she did?" Laurent asked.

"I am now," she admitted, "though I had doubts at the beginning. What about you, Laurent? What do you want your future to be like?"

"I know I'm destined to rule," Laurent began, choosing his words carefully. "The thought sometimes frightens me. I hope my father lives to a very old age so I'll have enough experience when I take the throne."

"It will be challenging," Elizabeth agreed.

"I will have to marry someday to secure the succession. But hopefully my bride will be someone I know and love." He touched her hair gently and turned her chin up so he could look deeply into her eyes. "Maybe in two or three years I will come to see you in your Sweet Valley."

Elizabeth's blue-green eyes sparkled at his words, and she smiled.

"I would like that very much. Anything is possible, Laurent," she said. He was unable to resist her lips, and she returned his kiss with all the passion he had come to expect.

"Yes," he said softly as he pulled away reluctantly, "anything is possible."

Elizabeth flung her arms around Laurent's neck, laughing and crying at the same time. "Oh, Laurent, whatever else happens, you'll always be my knight in shining armor!"

Chapter 14

"I can hardly believe we're on our way home," Elizabeth cried, watching as the scenery got smaller and smaller while the plane climbed through the clouds.

"Neither can I!" Jessica said, wriggling in her seat. She reached into the seat pocket in front of her and pulled out the in-flight magazine. "I can hardly wait to land."

"We have a few hours yet," Elizabeth said wryly.

Just then the flight attendant approached.

"Would either of you girls like a pillow?" she asked, smiling.

"Yes, please," Jessica said, reaching over her sister to accept the tiny pillow. Elizabeth shook her head no, and the flight attendant moved on.

"Maybe that's the job we should try for next summer," Jessica said.

"What job?" Elizabeth asked, her mind still half consumed by the memory of Laurent.

"Flight attendant, silly!" Jessica said, digging her elbow into Elizabeth's ribs. "Earth to Liz! Earth to Liz!"

"OK, OK," Elizabeth said dismissively. "But I don't think being a flight attendant is such a great idea, Jess. Don't you cause enough trouble on the ground?"

"Very funny," Jessica said with a phony pout. "So what do you want to do next summer?"

"Maybe try out that *Flair* job," Elizabeth said distractedly. She was happy to be heading for Sweet Valley, but there was no denying she was leaving a piece of herself behind. She would never forget Laurent—his kindness, his tenderness, and the warmth of his kisses.

"Think of the stories we have to tell everyone. Lila will be positively green when she finds out a prince asked you to marry him!" Jessica said gleefully.

Lila might be Jessica's best friend, but Elizabeth knew her sister enjoyed taking Lila down a peg once in a while. Elizabeth had to admit she enjoyed it too.

"Even the kids turned out to be OK," Elizabeth said, glad she could put away that stupid baby-sitter's guide forever.

"They got us out of the dungeon, didn't they?" Jessica and Elizabeth laughed together at the memory of sitting in the tiny cell in their ball gowns. How unreal it seemed now that they were on their way home!

"And Jacques," Elizabeth said. "Do you think you'll ever see him again?"

Jessica's eyes glazed over slightly. "I don't know," she said in a dreamy voice. "He was so romantic and mysterious and sexy . . . so French!"

Jessica reached down to her bag, stowed beneath the seat in front of her. She opened it, fished around for a moment, then pulled out her hand.

"I still have the pearl bracelet he gave me," she told Elizabeth, displaying it for her.

"It's so pretty," Elizabeth said, reaching out to touch the tiny beads. "But you know it's probably stolen. Why did you keep it?"

Jessica shrugged. "Something to remember him by." She fastened the clasp and shook her wrist, gazing at the bracelet in admiration. "I wonder if Laurent had anything to do with Jacques's escape. You know I asked him for help, right?"

"I thought so," Elizabeth admitted. "But when I asked Laurent, he wouldn't admit to anything. Do you think the prince and princess really meant it when they said they were glad we'd come?"

"Why wouldn't they be glad?" Jessica demanded. "We did a terrific job with those kids and solved the jewel mystery too!"

Elizabeth laughed. "You're right. Did you hear

about the countess when she left the château?"

"No," Jessica said, her eyes gleaming at the thought of gossip, as always.

"Anna told me the countess threatened to bad-mouth the prince and the princess to the press," Elizabeth said in a lowered voice. "When the prince pointed out that the press could easily find ways to be equally unkind to her, she turned purple and sputtered all the way out to the car."

When their fit of giggles over the countess had passed, Elizabeth found her thoughts even more on Sweet Valley.

"I wonder how Todd is doing," she said softly, a pang in her heart. "I love Laurent, but somehow Todd has been there in my heart too. I can't believe he didn't even bother to write."

Jessica winced at Elizabeth's words. It seemed like ages since she had thrown Todd's letter into the fire, and she had hoped the subject would never come up. She would rather be anywhere else at this moment, knowing she should come clean and confess what she had done. Still, it wasn't fair to deceive Elizabeth any longer.

"Liz, I have something to tell you," she began tentatively.

"What?" Elizabeth asked absently.

"I know you're not going to like it," Jessica continued, trying to put off the moment. She pulled at a loose thread on her seat, unraveling the upholstery. "I just hope you won't get too mad."

"What have you done now?" Elizabeth asked slowly.

"Well . . . um . . . actually it's nothing," Jessica said, chickening out. "Never mind. Just forget it."

"Are you kidding?" Elizabeth exclaimed. "You have to tell me now!"

"Um . . . uh . . ." Jessica was so scared, she was momentarily tongue-tied.

"Tell me!" Elizabeth demanded.

"Well, OK, but just remember, if you kill me, your life will be much less exciting," Jessica said, realizing that if Elizabeth got really mad, there wasn't anyplace she could run and hide on the plane. "Boy, I had no idea how hard this would be!"

"Just say it," Elizabeth prompted.

"Promise you won't get mad?" Jessica asked, hoping that Elizabeth would forgive her sometime this decade.

"Jessica," Elizabeth said in an exasperated voice, "you're really beginning to worry me here. What's going on?"

Jessica took a deep breath. "Todd did write," she said quietly. "But I burned the letter." She closed her eyes and hunched her shoulders slightly, waiting for the storm of Elizabeth's anger to hit.

After a moment she opened her eyes to look at her twin. Elizabeth was sitting openmouthed, her eyes widened in disbelief.

"You burned the letter?" she asked as if she didn't understand the words.

Jessica nodded, then took advantage of Elizabeth's shock. "I thought it was the right thing to do. You were so miserable about breaking up with him, and we had the whole summer ahead of us, and then there was Laurent. . . ." She trailed off lamely.

"You burned it," Elizabeth said again. Tears filled her eyes. "How could you do that to me?"

"It's all right, Liz, yell and scream at me if you want," Jessica said quickly, scared by Elizabeth's understated reaction.

"What a terrible thing to do," Elizabeth said, the tears falling freely now. She wiped them away with her hand and sat quietly for a moment, staring blankly at the seat in front of her. Jessica watched her sister in alarm, wondering when she would explode.

"But if you hadn't done it," Elizabeth said finally, slowly, "I might never have allowed myself to fall in love with Laurent."

"And you would have missed being proposed to by a prince!" Jessica said triumphantly. "So I actually did you a favor!"

"Don't get too smug," Elizabeth said warningly, but Jessica could tell she wasn't mad anymore.

She breathed an enormous sigh of relief and settled back in her seat, knowing that once again she had narrowly escaped disaster.

Much later that night Elizabeth and Todd walked along the beach, hand in hand. *This is where I belong,* Elizabeth thought. The familiar beating of the surf warmed her heart as she breathed in the sweet California air.

"I was sick with worry when you didn't write back," Todd was saying. "I was sure I'd made the biggest mistake of my life. I probably should have figured Jessica was at the bottom of it all."

"Hmmm," Elizabeth replied, unwilling to spoil the serenity she felt with too much talk.

"Hey," Todd said, his voice animated, "did you see much of the scandal that happened with the royal family while you were there?"

"Scandal?" Now Elizabeth was all ears. "What scandal?"

"It was all over the news here," Todd went on. "How the prince announced his engagement then canceled the whole thing. And there was some mystery girl no one knows about who the prince wanted to marry, but she turned him down. I can't believe you, with your reporter's instincts, didn't notice all that was going on."

"Oh, there was some excitement just before we left," Elizabeth said, coughing and clearing her throat in an effort not to burst out laughing. *Imagine if he knew that I'm the mystery girl!* she thought. "But you know, we were there to take care of the kids. That didn't leave time for much else," Elizabeth finished, amused at Todd's excitement over the scandal.

"Elizabeth." Todd's tone turned serious. "Can you ever forgive me for the way I acted before you left?"

Elizabeth turned to face him and looked deep into his warm brown eyes. She could see the love he felt for her, but she couldn't forget how devastated she'd been when she left for France.

"I don't know," she said honestly. "It really hurt to think that you might want to date someone else."

"There isn't any other girl in the world for me," he said passionately, clasping both her hands in his. "And I definitely don't want you to date other guys."

"Are you sure, Todd?" Elizabeth desperately wanted him to say yes, but she also wanted him to be honest. If he really didn't feel the same way about her, then she needed to know. She didn't want to be like Antonia, hanging on to a guy even though he didn't want her.

"Yes, Elizabeth, I'm absolutely sure," Todd stated. "Are you?"

She paused for a moment before replying. A memory of Laurent's handsome, chiseled features flitted through her mind. Elizabeth smiled slightly before pushing the image away. Laurent would always have a piece of her heart, but now that she was home, their love seemed as if it had been a dream. Todd's love was real, and he was here now, ready to open his heart to her.

"I'm sure," she answered honestly, smiling up into his handsome face. "All I want in the world is for us to be together." She cuddled closer to him, and he leaned down and kissed her passionately.

When they parted, Elizabeth pulled his arms around her waist and turned to look out at the water, leaning back against his chest. He nuzzled her neck with his lips, and Elizabeth smiled.

Todd is just as much a part of me now as he was before I left, she thought. *Now I'm truly home.*

The living room was silent as Jessica curled up in her favorite chair and stared out the window at the moon. In her hand she clutched the note Jacques had written to her, now worn around the edges from so many readings. She wondered if he was looking up at the same silver globe hanging in the black sky.

Out of the corner of her eye Jessica saw her mother enter the room.

"Are you still sitting here in the dark?" Mrs. Wakefield asked in an amused voice.

"Hmmm?" Jessica said, looking up.

"Never mind," Alice Wakefield said, waving her hand in dismissal and laughing. "Just let us know when you actually come home."

Jessica watched her mother leave. Maybe Jacques was even thinking of her right this instant, just as she was thinking of him.

"Jacques," she whispered into the empty room, "I miss you so much." Jessica shivered, imagining strong arms wrapped around her.

"Someday we'll meet again."

And in her heart she knew it to be true.

Jessica has left her fairy tale romance behind and is about to step into her worst nightmare! Find out what happens when the Sweet Valley High cheerleaders start to disappear . . . one by one. Don't miss the Sweet Valley High Super Thriller, **"R" for Revenge.** *It's the most shocking, terrifying, and twisted Super Thriller yet!*

Then, when a raging fire rips through Fowler Crest, Lila swears revenge on the arsonist who destroyed her life. Romantic sparks begin to fly between the most unlikely couple ever when Steven Wakefield is assigned to investigate the fire for the DA's office. Don't miss a moment of the scorching passion in Sweet Valley High #135, **Lila's New Flame,** *the first book in a three-part miniseries that will melt your heart!*

Bantam Books in the Sweet Valley High series
Ask your bookseller for the books you have missed